CONTENTS

Hichamou Prince' Professional Background — v

The Legend of Ziarani's Hidden Treasure — 1

The Enchanted Lineage of Ngazidja — 7

The Forbidden Salt Lake of Ngazidja — 13

The Enchanted Lake of Dzialandze — 19

The Brave Dog and the Jinn — 24

The Tale of Musa Mudu — 29

The Eel Treasure of Sima — 34

The Sultan of anjouan and the Enigmatic Sea Djinn — 39

The Herdsman and the Enchanted Beings
of the Forest — 46

The Majesty of Mount Ntringui and the
Marvels of anjouan — 52

The Barren Woman and the Vision of
The Strong Man — 58

The Poor Man of Mbadjini and the
Secret Treasure — 64

The Man From Mohéli and the
   Mermaid's Enchantment   70

The Man Who Dared to Defy God   76

The Wicked Witch and the Baby Who
   Overcame Her   82

The Mosque That Woke Mbadjini   87

The Tale of the Shadow Warrior and the
   Isles of Peace   92

The Wise Man and the Loyal Friend   97

The King and the Servant: A Tale of Love
   In Bimbini   101

The Selfish King and the Fall of His Kingdom   106

The Mystery of Guro Forest   111

The City of the Two Minarets   117

The Kindness of Sima: A Tale of Ba-Ibrahim   122

A Love Destined By Fate   126

A Love That Crossed Borders   132

Beyond the Surface   137

The Curse of Beauty   143

Beneath Divided Skies   149

From Outcast to Triumph   154

Eternal Love   158

Beyond Sight   163

The Heart's Decree   168

Between Two Hearts   173

From Betrayal to Triumph   177

Tales of the Comoros

Legends, Mysteries, and Enchantments
from the Isles of the Moon

Hichamou Prince

INDIA • SINGAPORE • MALAYSIA

ISBN
Paperback 9798897774616
Hardcase 9798897774623

HICHAMOU PRINCE' PROFESSIONAL BACKGROUND

Hichamou Prince is a proud native of the district of **Sima, Anjouan, in the Union of the Comoros**. A dedicated professional, passionate educator, and accomplished author; Prince has built a distinguished career rooted in a strong academic foundation and a commitment to personal and professional growth.

Early Education and Foundation

Prince's journey began in the heart of Sima, where he attended **Ecole Sima** II for his primary education. His early years were marked by a deep curiosity and a love for learning, traits that would define his future pursuits.

He continued his secondary education at **College Rural de Sima** and later completed his studies at **Multi-Language Private School**, where he developed a strong academic foundation and a global perspective.

Academic Achievements

Driven by a relentless ambition to excel, Prince pursued higher education with determination and focus. He earned a **Bachelor of Business Administration (BBA)** from **Team University**, where he gained a comprehensive understanding of business principles, leadership, and organizational dynamics. Building on this foundation, he completed a **Postgraduate Diploma in Human Resource Management (PGDHRM)** and furthered his expertise with a **Master of Science in Human Resource Management**. These qualifications have positioned him as a skilled professional in the field of human capital management, with a deep understanding of the strategies and practices that drive organizational success.

Professional Journey

Prince's professional journey is characterized by a commitment to excellence, innovation, and impact. His expertise in human resource management has enabled him to contribute meaningfully to his field, helping organizations optimize their workforce and achieve their goals. Beyond his professional accomplishments, Prince is deeply committed to community development, using his skills and knowledge to empower others and create opportunities for growth.

Personal Interests and Values

In addition to his academic and professional achievements, Prince is a man of diverse interests and passions. An avid reader, he finds inspiration and knowledge in literature, which fuels his intellectual curiosity and creative spirit. His love for football reflects his belief in teamwork, discipline, and the joy of collective achievement. These hobbies not only enrich his personal life but also inform his professional approach, emphasizing collaboration, resilience, and continuous learning.

A Legacy of Dedication and Impact

Hichamou Prince's journey is a testament to his resilience, dedication, and commitment to making a meaningful impact in his field and community. His story is one of perseverance, ambition, and an unwavering belief in the potential of individuals and communities to create a brighter future. As a professional, author, and proud Comorian, Prince continues to inspire others to dream boldly, work tirelessly, and contribute meaningfully to the world around them.

Hichamou Prince
Author
Human Resource Management Expert
Proud Comorian

THE LEGEND OF ZIARANI'S HIDDEN TREASURE

*I*n the heart of Sima District, nestled between rolling hills and fertile valleys, lay the village of Ziarani. It was a place of abundance, where the fields yielded golden grains, the rivers ran clear and cool, and the people lived in harmony with the land. The villagers were known for their hard work, their deep respect for tradition, and their unwavering unity. They were guided by the wisdom of their elders, who spoke of the blessings of the earth and the importance of protecting what they held dear.

But peace, as it often does, could not last forever.

Rumors began to spread of unrest in the East. A neighboring tribe, envious of Ziarani's prosperity, began to encroach on their lands. At first, it was small skirmishes—stolen livestock, burned crops—but soon, the tension escalated into a full-blown conflict. The men of Ziarani, proud and determined, prepared to defend their homeland. They sharpened their swords, fortified their village, and vowed to protect their families at all costs.

Yet, as the threat loomed closer, the elders made a difficult decision. They could not risk the lives of their women and children, nor could they allow their wealth—accumulated over generations—to fall into enemy hands. And so, a plan was devised.

Deep within the forest, hidden behind a waterfall and accessible only through a narrow, winding path, lay a secret cave. It was a place known only to the villagers, a sanctuary carved by nature itself. The women, children, and elders were sent there, along with the village's treasures—gold coins, precious jewels, and sacred artifacts. The men swore an oath: they would return for their loved ones once the conflict was over.

On the morning of the final battle, the men of Ziarani gathered in the village square. They prayed together, their voices rising in unison as they sought courage and strength. They kissed their children goodbye, embraced their wives, and promised to return victorious. Then, with heavy hearts, they marched to the battlefield.

But the enemy had been watching.

Unbeknownst to the men of Ziarani, their rivals had discovered the location of the cave. As the men knelt in prayer, the enemy forces launched a surprise attack. The battle was fierce and brutal. Swords clashed, arrows flew, and the air was thick with the cries of the wounded. Though the men of Ziarani fought valiantly, they were outnumbered. By nightfall, the battlefield was silent, littered with the fallen.

A handful of survivors managed to escape. Grief-stricken and battered, they fled to nearby villages, where they were taken in by sympathetic neighbors. These survivors would later become the foundation of the modern Sima District, carrying with them the memory of Ziarani's glory and tragedy.

But the story did not end there.

Days turned into weeks, and the cave remained eerily silent. The survivors, desperate to reunite with their families, ventured back to the hidden sanctuary. What they found was beyond comprehension.

The entrance to the cave was sealed, as if the earth itself had swallowed it whole. No amount of digging or force could open it. Strange whispers echoed through the forest, and those who lingered near the cave reported seeing flickering lights and shadowy figures moving in the darkness. The elders spoke in hushed tones of the jinn — mystical beings of immense power who had taken control of the cave.

"The jinn guard what is inside," they warned. "It is not for us to disturb."

Over the years, many brave souls attempted to uncover the secrets of the cave. Some sought the treasures; others hoped to find answers about their lost loved ones. But each attempt ended in failure. Those who entered never returned, and those who approached too closely were met with inexplicable phenomena—voices calling their names, sudden gusts of wind, and the feeling of being watched by unseen eyes.

One such adventurer was a young man named Karim, whose grandmother had been among those hidden in the cave. Determined to uncover the truth, Karim spent years studying the legends and consulting with mystics. Armed with ancient talismans and a heart full of hope, he ventured into the forest.

For three days and nights, Karim searched for the cave. On the fourth day, he found it—the entrance partially hidden by vines and moss. As he approached, the air grew colder, and the whispers grew louder. Ignoring the warnings of his elders, Karim stepped inside.

What he saw defied explanation. The cave was vast, its walls shimmering with an otherworldly light. Gold coins and jewels lay scattered on the ground, but they were untouched, as if frozen in time. In the center of the cave stood a figure—a woman cloaked in white, her face serene yet sorrowful.

"Why have you come?" she asked, her voice echoing like a distant melody.

Karim fell to his knees. "I seek the truth," he replied. "What happened to my people?"

The woman's eyes filled with tears. "They are at peace," she said. "The jinn have protected them, as they promised. But this place is not for the living. Go, and tell your people to honor the memory of Ziarani. Let the past rest."

Before Karim could respond, the cave began to tremble. The walls closed in, and the light faded. When he awoke, he was lying at the edge of the forest, the cave nowhere to be found.

Karim returned to his village and shared his story. Though some doubted him, most believed. The elders declared that the cave should remain undisturbed; a sacred place where the spirits of Ziarani's fallen could rest in peace.

Today, Ziarani is a place of quiet beauty and lingering mystery. The cave, now overgrown and hidden, remains a symbol of the village's resilience and the enduring power of its legacy. Travelers who pass through the area speak of strange occurrences — faint cries in the night, the glint of gold in the moonlight, and the feeling of being watched by unseen eyes.

The legend of Ziarani's hidden treasure lives on, a tale of bravery, loss, and the unbreakable bond between a people and their land. It is a reminder that some mysteries are meant to remain unsolved, and that the true treasure lies not in gold or jewels, but in the stories we pass down through generations.

And so, the people of Sima District honor the memory of Ziarani, their ancestors who fought and sacrificed for a better future. They tell the story to their children, ensuring that the spirit of Ziarani — its courage, its unity, and its enduring mystery — will never be forgotten.

THE ENCHANTED LINEAGE OF NGAZIDJA

*N*gazidja, the largest and most majestic island of the Comoros, was a place of unparalleled beauty. Its volcanic peaks pierced the sky, their slopes cloaked in emerald forests, while its shores were kissed by the turquoise waves of the Indian Ocean. But beyond its natural splendor, Ngazidja was a land steeped in mystery. The island's people spoke in hushed tones of the jinn — beings of fire and spirit, invisible yet ever-present, who were said to watch over the land.

For centuries, humans and jinns coexisted in an unspoken harmony. The jinns were believed to protect the island's prosperity, ensuring bountiful harvests and calm seas, while the humans lived their lives in reverence of these unseen guardians. Though the two worlds rarely intersected, there was a mutual respect that bound them together.

But one fateful evening, under the golden light of a setting sun, the boundary between the human and jinn worlds began to blur.

Amir was a young farmer, known throughout the village for his kindness and striking features. He spent his days tending to his fields near the edge of the forest, his hands calloused from work but his heart full of gratitude for the land that sustained him. He often sang as he worked, his voice carrying through the trees like a gentle breeze.

Unbeknownst to Amir, his songs had caught the attention of a jinn named Laila. She had watched him from the shadows of the forest, mesmerized by his gentle nature and the way he cared for the earth. Laila was unlike any other jinn — she was curious about the human world, drawn to its warmth and vitality. Over time, her fascination with Amir grew into something deeper.

One evening, as the sun dipped below the horizon, Laila decided to reveal herself. She stepped out of the forest, her form shimmering like moonlight on water. Amir, startled but not afraid, dropped his hoe and stared at her in awe. Laila's beauty was otherworldly, her eyes like pools of liquid gold, her presence both enchanting and humbling.

"Who are you?" Amir asked, his voice trembling with wonder.

"I am Laila," she replied, her voice like the rustle of leaves in the wind. "I have watched you, Amir, and I have come to know your heart. I wish to walk beside you, if you will have me."

Amir, though bewildered, felt an inexplicable connection to this ethereal being. He nodded, and from that day forward, Laila became a part of his life.

Their love was not without challenges. The villagers, though initially awed by Laila's presence, grew uneasy. They whispered of the dangers of mingling with the jinn, of ancient tales that warned against such unions. But Amir and Laila paid no heed to the rumors. Their bond was pure, a testament to the power of love to transcend boundaries.

In time, their family grew. Laila gave birth to three children—two daughters, Amina and Yasmin, and a son, Idris. Each child was extraordinary, bearing the mark of their dual heritage.

Amina, the eldest, had a gift for healing. Her touch could mend wounds and soothe ailments, and her presence brought comfort to the sick and weary. Yasmin, the second daughter, possessed a voice that seemed to hold the power of nature itself. When she sang, the winds would still, the rains would come, and the earth seemed to sigh in contentment. Idris, the youngest, was known for his strength and wisdom. Even as a child, he displayed an uncanny ability to resolve conflicts and bring people together.

The villagers marveled at the children, but not all were pleased. Some feared their powers, seeing them as a sign of the jinns' dominance. Others envied their gifts, whispering that such abilities were unnatural. Among the jinns, too, there was discontent. Some viewed Laila's decision to live among humans as a betrayal, a crossing of lines that should never have been crossed.

⁜ ⁜ ⁜

As tensions grew, Amir and Laila found themselves caught between two worlds. The humans demanded that Laila and her children prove their loyalty, while the jinns pressured Laila to return to their realm. It was a test of their love and their commitment to the life they had built together.

One night, as the family gathered around the fire, Idris spoke up. "Why must we choose?" he asked, his young voice steady and wise. "We are not just human or jinn. We are both. And that is our strength."

His words struck a chord. Amir and Laila realized that their children were not just a product of their love—they were a bridge between two worlds, a living testament to the harmony that could exist between humans and jinns.

Together, the family set out to mend the divide. Amina used her healing gifts to help the sick, proving that her powers were a blessing, not a curse. Yasmin sang to calm storms and bring rain to parched fields, showing the villagers that her voice was a force for good. Idris, with his wisdom, mediated disputes and brought people together, demonstrating that unity was possible.

Over time, the island of Ngazidja began to change. The humans and jinns, inspired by the family's efforts, learned to coexist openly. The island became a symbol of harmony, a place where the boundaries between worlds were not barriers but bridges.

✦ ✦ ✦

Years passed, and the family's legacy endured. Amina became a revered healer, her name spoken with gratitude by those she had helped. Yasmin's songs became a part of the island's folklore, passed down through generations. Idris grew into a wise leader, guiding the people of Ngazidja with compassion and fairness.

Even today, the people of Ngazidja tell the story of the enchanted lineage. They speak of Amir and Laila's love, a love that defied the boundaries of worlds. They tell of Amina's healing touch, Yasmin's songs that tamed storms, and Idris' wisdom that shaped their laws.

And as the sun sets over the island, casting its golden light over the volcanic peaks and lush forests, some say that if you listen closely, you can still hear the laughter of Laila and Amir's descendants. It is carried on the wind, a reminder that love and understanding can overcome even the deepest divides.

The jinns, too, have not forgotten. They watch over the island, their presence felt in the rustle of leaves and the flicker of firelight. And though they remain unseen, their bond with the humans endures, a silent promise that the harmony of Ngazidja will never be broken.

For on this island, where the earth meets the sky and the human world touches the realm of the jinn, the story of the enchanted lineage lives on—a tale of love, unity, and the magic that lies in the space between worlds.

THE FORBIDDEN SALT LAKE OF NGAZIDJA

*D*eep within the heart of Ngazidja Island, hidden behind jagged volcanic rocks and dense forests, lies a place of haunting beauty—a shimmering salt lake known as "The Lake of Whispers." Its waters glisten under the moonlight, reflecting the stars as if they were trapped within its depths. By day, the lake is still and silent, its surface a mirror to the sky. But by night, it comes alive with faint murmurs, as though the water itself is speaking.

The villagers of Ngazidja have long feared the lake. They speak of it in hushed tones, warning their children to stay far away. The elders say it is the domain of the jinn—mystical beings who guard its sacred waters. Some believe the lake is a portal between the human world and the realm of the jinn, while others whisper of treasures hidden beneath its surface, protected by powerful magic.

But the most chilling tale is this: anyone who dares to approach the lake never returns.

In a small village nestled at the foot of the island's volcanic peaks, there lived a young woman named Saida. She was unlike anyone else in the village — bold, curious, and unafraid of the unknown. While others avoided even the mention of the salt lake, Saida was drawn to it. She had grown up hearing the stories, and instead of fear, she felt a burning desire to uncover the truth.

Saida's curiosity only deepened one evening when her uncle, a respected storyteller, recounted an old legend. He spoke of a golden amulet hidden at the center of the lake, a relic said to grant immense power to whoever possessed it. The amulet was believed to be the key to the jinns' magic, a bridge between their world and the human realm.

"But beware," her uncle warned, his voice grave. "The lake is not a place for the living. Many have tried to find the amulet, and none have returned."

Saida listened intently, her heart racing. She couldn't shake the thought of the amulet and the secrets it might hold. That night, as she lay in bed, she made a decision.

She would find the amulet and uncover the truth about the lake.

⁕ ⁕ ⁕

On a moonlit night, Saida set out for the salt lake. She carried nothing but a lantern, a small knife, and her unyielding determination. The forest was eerily quiet, the only sound the crunch of leaves beneath her feet. As she drew closer to the lake, the air grew colder, and the whispers began.

At first, they were faint, like the rustle of leaves in the wind. But soon, they became voices — soft, melodic, and haunting.

"Turn back," they murmured. "This place is not for you."

Saida's heart pounded, but she pressed on. She had come too far to turn back now. When she reached the lake's edge, she was struck by its otherworldly beauty. The water shimmered like liquid silver, and the stars above seemed to dance on its surface.

But as she stepped closer, the ground beneath her feet gave way. Saida stumbled, her lantern falling from her hand as she plunged into the lake. Instead of sinking, she found herself in a vast, luminous cavern. The walls sparkled with crystals, casting a soft, ethereal glow. The air was thick with the scent of salt and something unearthly.

Before her stood a figure cloaked in light — a jinn. Its form was neither male nor female, its features shifting like the surface of the lake. Its eyes, deep and piercing, seemed to see straight into Saida's soul.

"Why have you come, human?" the jinn's voice echoed in her mind, both gentle and commanding. "This is a sacred place, forbidden to your kind."

Saida, though trembling, spoke with honesty. "I seek the truth about this lake and the amulet of legend."

The jinn regarded her for a long moment, its expression unreadable. Then it spoke again. "The amulet exists, but it is not what you think. It binds our worlds together, keeping balance and peace. If disturbed, chaos will reign."

To test Saida's intentions, the jinn showed her visions of what could happen if the amulet were removed — a world engulfed in storms, the jinn and humans at war, the island of Ngazidja torn apart by chaos. Saida's heart ached at the sight. She realized that her curiosity had blinded her to the consequences of her actions.

Humbled, Saida bowed her head. "I did not understand," she whispered. "I only wanted to know the truth."

The jinn's expression softened. "The truth is not always meant to be uncovered. Some mysteries exist to protect us."

Moved by Saida's sincerity, the jinn granted her safe passage back to her village. But it gave her one final warning: "You must protect the secret of the lake. Tell no one what you have seen, and ensure that no one else disturbs its waters."

✛ ✛ ✛

Saida returned to her village, forever changed by her journey. She never spoke of what she had seen in the jinns' realm, but her demeanor shifted. She became a storyteller, weaving tales that both intrigued and warned others of the lake's power.

Her stories were filled with caution, reminding the villagers of the delicate balance between their world and the realm of the jinn. She spoke of the beauty of the lake, but also of its dangers, ensuring that the legend of the forbidden salt lake would endure.

Over time, Saida became known as the guardian of the lake's secret. Though she never returned to its shores, she felt its presence always, a reminder of the responsibility she carried.

✛ ✛ ✛

To this day, the salt lake remains untouched, its secrets guarded by whispers and the memory of Saida's journey. The villagers still speak of the brave young woman who ventured to the lake and returned, forever changed.

And as the moon rises over Ngazidja, casting its silver light on the shimmering waters, some say they can still hear the faint murmurs of the lake—a reminder of the balance it upholds and the mysteries it protects.

For Saida, the lake was not just a place of danger, but a symbol of the unseen forces that shape their world. And though she never found the golden amulet, she discovered something far greater: the wisdom to respect the unknown and the courage to protect it.

THE ENCHANTED LAKE OF DZIALANDZE

In the heart of Anjouan Island, nestled within a lush, ancient forest, lies the tranquil lake of Dzialandze. Its crystal-clear waters reflect the sky like a perfect mirror, creating a scene of serene beauty. The air around the lake is filled with the melodies of birdsong, a symphony that seems to echo the harmony of nature itself. But beneath this idyllic surface lies a mystery that has captivated the people of Anjouan for generations.

The elders of the island speak of the lake's magical charm. No matter the season, no leaf, twig, or debris ever sullies its surface. This is not the work of nature alone, they say, but the result of the vigilant guardianship of the jinn — mystical beings who dwell within the lake and protect its purity.

Among the lake's many wonders are its birds. These are no ordinary creatures. Their feathers shimmer like silver in the sunlight, and their songs carry an otherworldly melody. The villagers believe these birds are servants of the jinn, tasked with maintaining the lake's pristine beauty. Whenever a leaf falls from the surrounding trees, the birds swoop down with astonishing speed, catching it mid-air and carrying it away before it can touch the water.

This phenomenon has made Dzialandze a place of wonder and reverence. Travelers from distant lands come to witness the spectacle, but none dare disturb the lake. Stories of those who tried and never returned keep the curious at bay.

In a small village near the lake, there lived a young boy named Hani. He was known for his boundless curiosity and mischievous spirit. While other children listened to the elders' warnings with wide-eyed fear, Hani was fascinated by the tales of the lake and its mystical guardians. He spent hours imagining what it would be like to see the jinn or to witness the birds in action.

One evening, as Hani sat by the fire listening to his grandmother recount the legend of Dzialandze, he made a decision. He would uncover the truth about the lake. Ignoring his grandmother's stern warnings, he crept out of the house at dawn, his heart pounding with excitement.

Hani made his way to the lake, hiding among the bushes near its edge. The morning air was cool, and the first light of dawn painted the sky in hues of pink and gold. As he watched, a leaf drifted down from a towering tree. Just as it was about to touch the water, a bird appeared in a flash of silver, catching the leaf and flying away.

Hani's eyes widened in amazement. The stories were true! But his curiosity was not satisfied. He wanted to see more. Plucking a handful of leaves from a nearby tree, he threw them into the air.

The birds reacted instantly, darting through the air to catch every single leaf. But as they did, the lake's waters began to ripple, and a strange mist rose from its surface. Hani's heart raced as a figure emerged from the mist—a jinn cloaked in light, with eyes that gleamed like the moon.

The jinn's voice was calm but firm. "Child, why do you disturb the peace of Dzialandze?"

Hani, trembling, managed to reply, "I… I wanted to see if the stories were true."

The jinn nodded, their gaze softening. "Curiosity is not a sin, but this lake is sacred. It remains pure because of our bond with the birds, who carry away what does not belong. Respect this harmony, and you shall always find peace here. Disrupt it, and you invite chaos."

Hani bowed his head in shame. "I'm sorry," he whispered. "I didn't mean to cause harm."

The jinn's expression softened further. "You are young, and your heart is full of wonder. But remember, some mysteries are meant to be respected, not unraveled. Go now, and share this lesson with your people."

With that, the jinn vanished, and the mist retreated, leaving the lake as calm and pristine as before.

Hani returned to the village, his heart heavy with guilt but also filled with a newfound sense of purpose. He gathered the villagers and shared his story, his voice trembling as he recounted his encounter with the jinn.

The villagers listened in awe, their fear of the lake mingling with a deeper respect for its guardians. Hani's grandmother placed a hand on his shoulder and said, "You have learned a valuable lesson, my child. The lake is not just a place of beauty — it is a reminder of the balance between our world and the unseen forces that protect it."

From that day forward, the people of the village held Dzialandze in even greater reverence. They taught their children the story of Hani and the jinn, ensuring that the lake's tranquility would never be disturbed.

Years passed, and Hani grew into a wise and respected member of the community. He often visited the lake, not to test its mysteries, but to sit by its shores and reflect on the lessons he had learned. The birds continued their silent guardianship, their silver feathers glinting in the sunlight as they carried away fallen leaves.

Travelers still came from far and wide to witness the wonder of Dzialandze, but they did so with respect, mindful of the stories that surrounded the lake. The legend of Hani and the jinn became a cherished part of Anjouan's folklore, a reminder of the harmony that can exist when humans honor the sacred mysteries of their world.

And so, the enchanted lake of Dzialandze remains as pure as ever, its waters untouched by the passage of time. The birds sing their otherworldly melodies, and the jinn watch over the lake, their presence felt in the rustle of leaves and the shimmer of the water.

For Hani, the lake was not just a place of beauty, but a symbol of the delicate balance between curiosity and respect, between the seen and the unseen. And as he sat by its shores, listening to the songs of the silver-feathered birds, he knew that some mysteries were best left undisturbed.

THE BRAVE DOG
AND THE JINN

*I*n a small, quiet village nestled between rolling hills and fertile fields, there lived a mother and her newborn baby. Their home was a modest hut made of clay and straw, surrounded by a small farm where goats, cows, and chickens roamed. The mother, a hardworking woman named Amina, spent her days tending to the farm and caring for her child. Her baby, a rosy-cheeked boy named Yusuf, was the light of her life. She would sing lullabies to him as he slept, her voice filling the room with warmth and love.

But one sunny morning, everything changed.

Amina had left Yusuf sleeping in his cradle while she went to tend to the fields. The morning air was crisp, and the sun cast a golden glow over the village. As she worked, a strange feeling crept over her — a sense of unease that she couldn't shake. Hurrying back to the house, she froze at the sight before her.

Inside the room, a dark figure loomed over the cradle. It was a jinn, its form shadowy and indistinct, with glowing eyes that burned like embers. The air around it seemed to shimmer with an unnatural heat. The jinn turned its gaze toward Amina and hissed, "Leave now, or you will never see your child again."

Amina's heart pounded with fear and desperation. She knew the jinn was powerful, but she couldn't abandon her baby. Her mind raced as she tried to think of a way to save Yusuf. Then, an idea struck her — she would call for help from the animals on her farm.

+ + +

Amina ran to the goat, who was grazing peacefully nearby. "Oh, dear goat," she pleaded, "please help me! There's a jinn in my house threatening my baby. Come and chase it away!"

The goat, loyal and gentle, agreed without hesitation. It trotted to the house and stood at the door, letting out a loud bleat. "Baa! Baa! Leave this house at once, or face me!"

The jinn sneered, its voice dripping with malice. "If you dare to step inside, I will eat you alive."

The goat, terrified by the jinn's menacing presence, turned and fled. It ran back to the farm and found the cow, who was chewing cud under the shade of a tree. "Cow, you must help!" the goat cried. "There's a jinn in the house, and the baby is in danger!"

The cow, known for its strength and calm demeanor, agreed to help. It stomped to the house, its hooves thudding against the ground. Standing at the doorway, it bellowed, "Moo! Moo! Leave this place, or face my wrath!"

The jinn laughed a sound that sent shivers down the cow's spine. "If you enter this room, I will devour you piece by piece," it warned.

The cow, unnerved by the jinn's threat, backed away and returned to the farm. It found the cat lounging in a patch of sunlight and said, "Cat, you must go to the house! A jinn is threatening the baby, and we need your help!"

The cat, though small, was quick and clever. It darted to the house and perched at the window, peering inside. With a loud "Mew! Mew!" it called out to the jinn, "Leave this house, or you'll regret it!"

The jinn's eyes narrowed, and its voice grew cold. "If you come any closer, I will swallow you whole."

The cat, sensing the danger, decided it was no match for the jinn. It sprinted back to the farm and found the dog resting under a tree. "Dog, you are brave and strong.

The baby is in danger! A jinn is in the house, and only you can save the child!"

⁜ ⁜ ⁜

The dog, a sturdy and loyal creature named Simba, leapt to its feet. Its ears perked up, and its eyes blazed with determination. Without hesitation, it ran to the house, its tail held high. Standing at the doorway, it growled fiercely, baring its sharp teeth. "Grrr! Grrr! Leave this house, or face my bite!"

The jinn glared at the dog, its glowing eyes narrowing. "If you enter this room, I will kill you," it hissed.

But Simba did not falter. It charged into the room, barking loudly and snapping its jaws. The jinn, startled by the dog's courage and ferocity, hesitated. Simba lunged at the jinn, forcing it to retreat. The jinn let out a final, furious cry before vanishing into thin air, leaving behind a faint smell of sulfur.

⁜ ⁜ ⁜

The room was silent once more. Yusuf, still safe in his cradle, cooed softly as Amina rushed inside. She scooped up her child, tears of relief streaming down her face. Turning to Simba, she knelt and hugged the dog tightly.

"You are our hero," she said, her voice trembling with emotion. "Thank you for saving my baby."

Simba wagged its tail, panting happily as if to say, "I would do it again."

From that day on, Simba was celebrated as a protector and a symbol of bravery. Amina told the story of the brave dog and the jinn to everyone in the village, and the tale spread far and wide. The villagers began to see dogs in a new light, not just as guardians of their homes but as loyal companions willing to risk everything for those they loved.

As for Simba, it became a beloved figure in the village. Children would bring it treats, and elders would pat its head, murmuring words of gratitude. Amina and Yusuf, in particular, shared a special bond with the dog. They would often sit together under the tree where Simba liked to rest, the mother singing lullabies to her son as the dog lay at their feet, its ears twitching contentedly.

The story of the brave dog and the jinn was passed down through generations, a reminder of the courage that lies within even the humblest of hearts. And though the jinn was never seen again, the villagers never forgot the lesson it had taught them: that love and loyalty can overcome even the darkest of threats.

And so, in that small, quiet village, the legend of Simba lived on—a tale of bravery, devotion, and the unbreakable bond between a mother, her child, and their faithful dog.

THE TALE OF MUSA MUDU

*L*ong ago, in the heart of Anjouan Island in the Comoros, there was a small, bustling settlement surrounded by lush forests and sparkling blue waters. The people of the settlement lived simple lives, farming, fishing, and trading with neighboring villages. They were content, but their lives were modest, and they often struggled to make ends meet.

One day, a mysterious traveler arrived in the village. His name was Musa, and he was unlike anyone the villagers had ever seen. Musa was tall and strong, with skin as dark as the night sky. His eyes gleamed with wisdom, and his voice carried the weight of distant lands. The villagers were curious about this stranger, but also cautious. They whispered among themselves, calling him "Musa Mudu," which in Shikomori meant "Musa is black."

Musa did not mind the whispers. Instead, he greeted the villagers warmly and offered to share stories of his travels. He spoke of vast deserts where the sun burned like fire, towering mountains that touched the clouds, and oceans that stretched beyond the horizon. The villagers listened in awe, their imaginations ignited by Musa's words.

But Musa's true gift was his knowledge of trade. He had traveled to many lands and learned the secrets of barter and commerce. Seeing the potential in the settlement, Musa began to teach the villagers how to trade more effectively. He showed them how to preserve their fish for longer journeys, how to weave baskets that were prized in other markets, and how to build boats sturdy enough to sail to neighboring islands.

At first, the villagers were hesitant. Change was unfamiliar, and they were unsure if they could trust this stranger. But Musa was patient. He worked alongside them, demonstrating his techniques and sharing his knowledge freely. Slowly, the villagers began to see the benefits of his teachings.

One day, Musa gathered the villagers and said, "You have everything you need to thrive—fertile land, skilled hands, and a spirit of community. But to truly prosper, you must look beyond your shores. The world is vast, and it is filled with opportunities."

Inspired by Musa's words, the villagers began to expand their trade. They built larger boats and ventured to distant islands, bringing back exotic goods like spices, fabrics, and precious stones. Traders from other lands began to visit the settlement, drawn by the quality of its products and the warmth of its people.

The village grew into a bustling trade center, with markets filled with colorful fabrics, fragrant spices, and treasures from across the seas. The villagers, who once struggled to make ends meet, now prospered. They built new homes, established schools, and celebrated their newfound wealth with festivals and feasts.

The name "Musa Mudu" began to take on a new meaning. It was no longer just a description of the traveler; it became a symbol of transformation and prosperity. The villagers began to call their growing town "Mutsamudu," in honor of the man who had brought them together and shown them the path to success.

✛ ✛ ✛

One evening, as the villagers gathered around a bonfire to celebrate their achievements, Musa shared a legend with them. He spoke of a rare black pearl hidden in the depths of the ocean, a pearl said to bring great fortune to whoever found it.

"The pearl is not just a treasure," Musa explained. "It is a symbol of courage, unity, and the rewards that come from daring to dream."

The villagers, inspired by the story, decided to embark on a grand expedition to search for the pearl.

They built a magnificent ship, named "Mudu's Grace," and set sail under Musa's leadership.

For weeks, they braved storms and navigated treacherous waters. Musa's wisdom and courage guided them, and the villagers grew stronger and more united. Finally, they arrived at a mysterious island shrouded in mist. There, in a hidden cove, they found the black pearl, glistening like a star in the darkness.

The villagers returned home as heroes, with the black pearl as a symbol of their journey. Musa placed the pearl in the center of the town square, where it became a source of inspiration for all who saw it. People from across the islands came to see the pearl and hear the story of Mutsamudu's transformation.

As the years passed, Musa grew older, but his spirit remained strong. He spent his days teaching the children of Mutsamudu, ensuring that his knowledge and values would be passed down to future generations.

One morning, the villagers awoke to find that Musa had disappeared. Some say he sailed away to explore new lands, while others believe he returned to the heavens, his mission on earth complete. In his absence, the villagers vowed to honor his memory by continuing to build on the foundation he had laid.

Today, Mutsamudu is a thriving town, known as the trade hub of Anjouan Island. Its markets buzz with activity, its harbor welcomes ships from distant lands, and its people carry forward the legacy of the man who taught them to see beyond their horizons.

The black pearl still sits in the town square, a reminder of Musa's wisdom and the journey that brought the villagers together. The tale of Musa Mudu is told to every child, a story of courage, unity, and the power of dreams.

And so, the spirit of Musa lives on, not just in the name of the town, but in the hearts of its people. They remember the stranger who came to their village with nothing but his wisdom and his stories, and who showed them that even the smallest beginnings can lead to the grandest transformations.

For in the heart of Mutsamudu, Musa's spirit shines as brightly as the black pearl that symbolizes his journey — a beacon of hope, inspiration, and the enduring power of community.

THE EEL TREASURE OF SIMA

*L*ong ago, in the coastal region of Sima District on the island of Anjouan, the people lived in harmony with the ocean. The sea was their lifeblood, providing food, trade, and a sense of identity. Every morning, the fishermen of Sima would set out in their wooden boats, casting their nets with skill and patience. They respected the ocean, knowing it could be both generous and unforgiving.

One fateful day, a fierce storm rolled in from the horizon. The sky darkened, and the waves rose like mountains, crashing against the shore with a fury that sent the villagers scrambling for safety. The fishermen hurried back to land, their boats barely making it to the safety of the beach. When the storm finally passed, the villagers emerged to assess the damage.

Among the debris left by the storm, something unusual caught their attention. In a shallow tide pool, a sleek, sinuous creature wriggled in the sunlight. It was an eel, but unlike any they had ever seen. Its skin shimmered with iridescent hues, and it moved with an almost magical grace. The villagers gathered around, murmuring in awe and uncertainty.

The elders of the village were called to examine the creature. "It might be a gift from the sea," one elder said, his voice filled with reverence. Another, more cautious, warned, "It could be a curse. We must be careful."

Among the villagers was a brave fisherman named Hamadi. Known for his curiosity and adventurous spirit, Hamadi stepped forward. "Let me take it home," he said. "I will cook it and see what it brings us."

That evening, Hamadi prepared the eel with care, seasoning it with herbs and spices from his garden. When he tasted it, he was astonished. The flavor was unlike anything he had ever experienced—rich, tender, and deeply satisfying. He shared the dish with his family, and soon, word spread throughout the village. The eel became a prized delicacy, and the elders declared it a blessing from the ocean, meant to nourish and strengthen the people of Sima.

☩ ☩ ☩

As generations passed, the eel became more than just a source of food. It became a symbol of prosperity and good fortune. Stories began to circulate about an Eel Spirit, a mystical guardian of the sea's treasures. The Eel Spirit, it was said, had chosen the people of Sima to honor her gift and protect her sacred creatures.

According to legend, the Eel Spirit would appear on nights when the moon was full, her shimmering form gliding through the water to bless the village. Those who respected her gift were rewarded with bountiful catches and calm seas. But those who disrespected the eel—or took more than they needed—would face her wrath.

The villagers took these stories to heart. They fished sustainably, ensuring that the eel population thrived. They held ceremonies to honor the Eel Spirit, offering prayers and gifts to show their gratitude. The eel became a cornerstone of their culture, a symbol of their connection to the sea and to each other.

✛ ✛ ✛

But not everyone heeded the warnings.

One day, a young fisherman named Mwana decided to test the legend. Unlike the others, he was skeptical of the stories. To him, the eel was just a source of food and profit. Determined to catch as many eels as possible, he ventured out to the reef alone, ignoring the warnings of the elders.

Mwana's net filled quickly, and he smiled at his success. But as he pulled the net from the water, the ocean grew eerily still. The waves ceased their gentle lapping, and the air became heavy with silence. Suddenly, a soft, glowing light emerged from the depths.

The Eel Spirit appeared before him, her form radiant and otherworldly. Her voice was gentle yet powerful: "Why do you take more than you need, young one? My gift is not for greed but for sustenance and culture."

Terrified, Mwana dropped his net and fell to his knees. "Forgive me," he pleaded. "I did not understand."

The Eel Spirit looked into his heart and saw his remorse. "Return what you do not need to the sea," she said, "and respect the balance of life. Teach others to honor this gift, or your village will face the consequences."

Mwana obeyed, releasing most of his catch back into the water. When he returned to the village, he shared his experience with the elders. They listened carefully and decided to make Mwana a messenger of the Eel Spirit's wisdom.

Over time, the eel became more than just a delicacy; it became a symbol of Sima's identity. The people of Sima took pride in their unique relationship with the eel, viewing it as a cultural treasure. Other regions in the Comoros marveled at their traditions, and visitors came from far and wide to witness the Festival of the Eel, a vibrant celebration of music, dance, and, of course, eel dishes.

The elders of Sima taught the younger generations to fish sustainably, ensuring that the eel population thrived. They believed that as long as they honored the Eel Spirit and respected the ocean, Sima would continue to prosper.

Today, the people of Sima remain the only ones in the Comoros who eat and value the eel. Their traditions have stood the test of time, passed down from one generation to the next. The eel is more than a delicacy; it is a symbol of resilience, respect, and unity.

The tale of the Eel Spirit lives on, a reminder of the harmony between humans and nature. And in the quiet waters off the shores of Sima, it is said that the Eel Spirit still watches over her people, shimmering under the light of the full moon.

For the people of Sima, the eel is not just a treasure of the sea — it is a treasure of the soul, a gift that binds them to their past, their present, and the endless rhythm of the ocean.

THE SULTAN OF ANJOUAN AND THE ENIGMATIC SEA DJINN

*O*nce upon a time, on the island of Anjouan, a land of emerald hills and shimmering waters, there ruled a wise and just Sultan named Ali. His kingdom was peaceful, and his people loved him for his kindness and fair rule. The palm trees swayed in the gentle breeze, the sun painted the sky with brilliant hues at dawn and dusk, and the sea stretched endlessly beyond the horizon, a vast expanse of blue and mystery.

But though Sultan Ali had everything a ruler could wish for — wealth, power, and the respect of his people — his heart was lonely. He longed for a companion, someone who could understand the depth of his soul and share his dreams. He spent many nights gazing at the stars, his thoughts wandering far beyond the comforts of his palace.

"What is a king without love?" he often wondered. He felt a deep emptiness, a yearning he could not ignore. For all his riches, he had no one to share his joys, no one to hear the whispers of his heart.

+ + +

One evening, as the sun set behind the waves, casting the world in golden light, the Sultan wandered alone to the shores of the island. The sky was painted with hues of orange and pink, and the gentle sea breeze whispered ancient songs from distant lands. Sultan Ali stood at the edge of the water, gazing out into the horizon, when suddenly, the air shimmered with a mysterious light.

From the depths of the sea rose a magnificent creature—a woman of such beauty that even the stars seemed to pale in comparison. Her long, flowing hair cascaded like liquid silver, the color of midnight under the moonlight, and her eyes sparkled like the brightest stars in the night sky. Her skin glowed with a faint luminescence, and the sound of her voice was like the soft murmur of the ocean itself, both soothing and powerful.

She was a Djinn, a spirit of the sea, a guardian of the depths, and her name was Laila. For centuries, she had lived in the heart of the ocean, watching over the waters and the creatures within. She was ancient, wise beyond measure, and yet, despite her power, she had grown weary of her solitary existence beneath the waves. The endless expanse of the ocean had begun to feel like a cage, and her heart ached for connection, for a bond beyond the cool, vast waters.

The Sultan, entranced by her beauty and the ethereal glow surrounding her, could not speak at first. He stood frozen, his breath caught in his throat, as Laila smiled, sensing the depth of his longing. She spoke softly, the words flowing like a gentle tide.

"Why do you wander alone, Sultan of Anjouan?" she asked. "Your kingdom is rich, your people are happy, but your heart is heavy with loneliness. You are a ruler, yet you carry a burden greater than any crown—a heart unfulfilled."

The Sultan, overcome by her presence, found the courage to speak. His voice was a whisper, as if the very wind could carry away his words.

"I have everything a ruler could want," he confessed, "but my heart yearns for a love that transcends all earthly possessions. I seek a soul that can truly understand mine, one who can share my hopes, my dreams, my very essence."

Laila's eyes softened with compassion, for she knew the pain of solitude. She too had wandered in search of something deeper, something beyond the eternal rhythm of the sea. As the waves lapped gently at the shore, a connection was formed between the Sultan and the

Djinn—a bond of deep understanding, a silent promise between two souls who had longed for one another.

"I have watched over the seas for countless years," Laila said, her voice barely more than a whisper, "but I have never known the warmth of a human heart. I have never shared the joys and sorrows of a mortal life. Perhaps, Sultan Ali, it is time for me to step into your world."

Filled with admiration and love for the Djinn, the Sultan knelt before her and offered his heart.

"Will you be mine, and join me in my life on land?" he asked. "Let me show you the beauty of the world beyond the waves. Together, we could build a life that transcends the heavens and the earth."

Laila, who had never known the warmth of human love, hesitated. She was a Djinn, bound to the sea by ancient magic, a spirit of water and wind. But the sincerity in the Sultan's eyes was undeniable, and she sensed a depth of love in him that was rare and precious. After a long pause, she spoke, her voice tinged with both longing and caution.

"I will join you, Sultan Ali," she said, "but there is a price to be paid. I will live with you on land for as long as you keep the love in your heart true. If ever you forget the depth of our bond, or let the warmth of your heart grow cold, I will return to the sea, and we shall be apart forever."

The Sultan, filled with joy, swore that he would never let their love fade. And so, Laila stepped onto the land, taking on the form of a beautiful woman, her ethereal glow dimming slightly as she embraced her new life among mortals. Together, she and Sultan Ali ruled Anjouan with wisdom and grace. The kingdom flourished under their reign, as the people admired the strength and unity between the Sultan and the Djinn. Sultan Ali's heart was no longer heavy, for he had found the one who truly understood him.

—†— —†— —†—

For many years, their love was a beacon of light in the kingdom. The sun rose and set, the seasons changed, and life went on, filled with laughter, love, and prosperity. But as the years passed, the Sultan's duties as a ruler grew heavier. The demands of the throne, the affairs of the kingdom, and the endless challenges of leadership began to cloud his heart. The once-vibrant connection he shared with Laila began to wane, overshadowed by the weight of his responsibilities.

One fateful evening, as the Sultan walked along the shores of Anjouan, he noticed that the sea, which had once been calm and welcoming, had become dark and turbulent. The waves crashed angrily against the rocks, and the air seemed thick with sorrow. A cold chill filled his heart, and he knew, deep down, that something was wrong.

Then, from the sea, Laila appeared before him once more. Her eyes were filled with sorrow, and her form shimmered with an ethereal glow that now seemed faint, as though it were fading.

"Sultan Ali," she said softly, her voice laced with sadness, "your heart has grown distant. The love we shared has begun to fade, and I can feel the coldness creeping into your soul. I must return to the sea."

The Sultan's heart broke in an instant. He realized too late the weight of his neglect, the time he had spent lost in the demands of his kingdom, and the distance he had placed between himself and the woman he loved.

"No, Laila, please!" he pleaded, his voice shaking. "I swear to you, I have never stopped loving you. I was lost, but I see now that you are the light of my life. I will never forget our bond again."

But Laila, though filled with love for him, knew the laws of her spirit. She could not remain where the love was not pure. "The sea calls me, Sultan," she said, "and I must return. But know this—true love never truly ends. It lingers in the hearts of those who have known it, and though we may be apart, our bond shall never break. You will always carry a part of me within you."

With that, Laila vanished into the waves, leaving behind only the faintest trace of her glow. Sultan Ali stood alone on the shore, his heart aching with the loss of the Djinn he had once loved.

From that day forward, the Sultan ruled with a wisdom born of his loss. He never forgot Laila, and he never allowed his heart to grow cold again. He became a ruler who deeply understood the value of love and connection. The people of Anjouan whispered that on quiet nights, when the moon was high and the waves were calm, they could see a faint glow on the horizon—Laila, watching over her beloved Sultan, guarding his heart from afar.

And so, the Sultan of Anjouan learned that love, once found, is a treasure that must be cared for and cherished. Even the mighty Sultan could not control the tides of the heart, but he knew that love, like the sea, would always return when it was true.

And in the silence of the night, when the waves whispered their songs, Sultan Ali knew that Laila's love would always be with him—forever, like the endless ocean.

The tale of the Sultan and the Sea Djinn became a legend, passed down through generations as a reminder of the power of love, the importance of balance, and the enduring connection between the human heart and the mysteries of the sea.

THE HERDSMAN AND THE ENCHANTED BEINGS OF THE FOREST

*O*nce upon a time, in a peaceful village nestled between rolling hills and vast forests, there lived a humble herdsman named Yassin. He was a man of simple means, living off the land and tending to his flock of goats. Every morning, he would rise with the sun, whistle a tune, and lead his goats to graze in the meadows. His life was modest, and though he worked hard, he often dreamed of something greater — of wealth, comfort, and a life beyond the fields.

Yassin was well-loved in the village for his kindness and his gentle nature. He would often share his milk and cheese with those in need, and his laughter could brighten even the gloomiest of days. But deep down, he carried a quiet longing, a yearning for a life that felt just out of reach.

One morning, as the sun rose over the horizon, Yassin decided to venture deeper into the forest than he ever had before. He had heard whispers from the villagers about the forest's secrets—ancient magic, strange creatures, and hidden treasures. Though he had always dismissed these stories as mere superstition, something stirred within him that day. A sense of adventure, a pull in his heart, urged him to explore the unknown.

✦ ✦ ✦

As Yassin walked deeper into the woods, the trees grew taller, their branches intertwining to form a canopy that filtered the sunlight into golden beams. The air grew cooler, and the sounds of the village faded away, replaced by the rustling of leaves and the occasional chirp of a bird. Soon, the forest grew eerily quiet, as if holding its breath.

Yassin found himself in a clearing unlike any place he had ever seen. The ground was carpeted with soft moss, and the air shimmered with a faint, otherworldly light. In the center of the clearing, he noticed small figures—creatures no larger than his hand, their skin glowing with a soft, ethereal glow. They looked like tiny humans, with delicate features and eyes that sparkled like stars. They moved with grace and purpose, as though they were guardians of the forest.

The creatures looked up as Yassin approached, and without fear, they beckoned him closer. One of them, with eyes as bright as the stars, stepped forward. In its left hand, it held a small pouch filled with glittering coins — golden money that shone with an otherworldly glow. In its right hand, it held a simple, coiled rope, weathered and worn but sturdy.

The tiny creature spoke in a voice that was both soothing and wise. "Choose wisely, herdsman. In my left hand is wealth beyond measure — gold, jewels, and riches. In my right hand is a rope, simple but powerful, a tool that can take you to places money cannot. Choose one, and the path you walk will forever change."

Yassin was struck by the choice before him. The gold gleamed enticingly in the creature's left hand, and the promise of riches stirred his heart. But he paused, sensing something deeper in the creature's words. He had lived a life of simplicity, and although wealth was tempting, he wondered if the rope might offer something more — a way to improve his life in a way that no amount of gold could.

After a long moment of thought, Yassin made his decision. With a humble nod, he chose the rope.

The creatures did not speak again, but instead, they handed him the coiled rope and vanished into the forest, their tiny forms disappearing like whispers in the wind. Yassin, though bewildered, left the forest and returned home to his village, the rope slung over his shoulder.

Days turned into weeks, and Yassin's life remained as it had always been—quiet, simple, and filled with the routine of tending to his goats. But one morning, as he prepared to take his herd out to graze, he noticed something strange. When he took the rope and tied it to a tree to secure his goats, the rope seemed to shimmer and grow stronger in his hands. He gave it a tug, and suddenly, a path appeared before him, leading deep into the heart of the forest.

Curious, Yassin followed the path. The rope guided him effortlessly through the dense trees, leading him to a hidden grove where wild fruits and herbs grew in abundance, far more than he could ever harvest in a lifetime. He realized that the rope had not only led him to this magical place but had also gifted him with the knowledge of how to cultivate the land around him. With time, he learned how to weave the rope into nets, traps, and even tools that made his work easier.

✦ ✦ ✦

Months passed, and with the help of the rope and the gifts of the forest, Yassin's farm flourished. He gathered the wild fruits and herbs, traded them with the villagers, and soon his name was known far and wide. He became wealthy in ways that money alone could not achieve—through his knowledge of nature, his hard work, and the help of the enchanted rope. His goats multiplied, his lands grew fertile, and his house became a home of abundance.

As the years went by, Yassin's wealth surpassed that of the richest merchants in the village. He built a beautiful home, planted orchards, and became a generous benefactor to those in need. But despite his newfound prosperity, he never forgot the simple life he had once known. He continued to work with his hands, using the rope to help others, sharing his wisdom and the secrets of the forest with those who sought his counsel.

One day, as he sat in his garden, watching the sun dip below the horizon, Yassin reflected on the choice he had made all those years ago. He realized that while the gold would have brought him riches, it was the rope that had truly transformed his life. The rope had given him more than wealth—it had given him the ability to create, to grow, and to live in harmony with nature.

And so, the humble herdsman who had once dreamed of riches became the wealthiest man in the village—not through gold, but through the simple yet powerful choice of a rope that had led him to a life of abundance, wisdom, and fulfillment.

The villagers often asked Yassin about the secret to his success, and he would smile, holding up the worn, coiled rope. "This," he would say, "is not just a rope. It is a reminder that true wealth lies not in what we have, but in what we do with what we are given."

And so, the tale of Yassin and the enchanted beings of the forest became a legend, passed down through generations as a reminder of the power of humility, wisdom, and the magic that lies within the simplest of choices.

In the quiet moments of his life, Yassin would often return to the forest, the rope in hand, and sit in the clearing where he had first met the tiny creatures. Though he never saw them again, he felt their presence in the rustling of the leaves and the shimmering of the light. And he knew that, in choosing the rope, he had chosen a path that would forever connect him to the magic of the forest and the wisdom of the earth.

THE MAJESTY OF MOUNT NTRINGUI AND THE MARVELS OF ANJOUAN

*O*nce upon a time, on the island of Anjouan in the heart of the Comoros, there stood a majestic mountain known as Ntringui. Towering above the island, its peak seemed to touch the sky, and its slopes were covered in dense forests, cascading waterfalls, and mysterious caves. The people of Anjouan spoke of the mountain in hushed tones, for it was said that Ntringui was not just a mountain, but a place of magic and wonder, filled with secrets that could change the lives of those brave enough to seek them.

Legends told of strange creatures that lived in its forests, of streams that flowed with waters of pure gold, and of flowers that bloomed once every hundred years, granting wishes to those who were pure of heart. But the most extraordinary of all was the tale of the Mountain Spirit, a powerful and wise being that lived at the very summit of Ntringui. It was said that the Spirit could grant one wish to anyone who reached the top of the mountain, but only if their heart was truly worthy.

For generations, people had tried to climb Ntringui, drawn by the promise of its wonders. Many had failed, for the path to the summit was treacherous and filled with challenges that tested the very soul of the climber. Some turned back, others were lost to the wilds of the mountain, but the mountain remained untouched, its mysteries concealed from the world below.

In a small village at the foot of Ntringui, there lived a young girl named Amina. She was known throughout the village for her kindness and courage. Amina had grown up listening to the stories of Ntringui, told by her grandmother under the light of the moon. Her grandmother would say, "The mountain is not just a place, Amina. It is a test of the heart. Only those who seek not for themselves, but for others, can unlock its magic."

Amina's village was poor, and life was hard. The people struggled to grow enough food, and the children often went to bed hungry. Amina's heart ached for her people, and she dreamed of finding a way to help them. One day, as she stood at the edge of the village, gazing up at the towering peak of Ntringui, she made a decision.

She would climb the mountain and seek the Mountain Spirit's blessing.

Her family and friends tried to dissuade her. "The mountain is dangerous," they said. "Many have tried and failed. What makes you think you can succeed?"

But Amina was determined. "I may not be the strongest or the bravest," she replied, "but my heart is true. I will climb Ntringui not for myself, but for all of us."

✦ ✦ ✦

With a heart full of hope and determination, Amina set off on her journey early one morning, leaving behind her family and friends. As she ascended the lower slopes of Ntringui, she encountered her first challenge: a dark, tangled forest, its trees thick with vines and shadow. The air was heavy, and the forest seemed alive, whispering ancient secrets.

Amina pushed forward, her heart full of resolve. After hours of walking, she came across a clearing where a great stone statue stood, depicting a fierce lion. It was said that the statue was enchanted, guarding the entrance to the deeper parts of the mountain. Amina felt a surge of bravery and approached the statue, whispering a prayer for guidance.

Suddenly, the ground trembled, and the lion's eyes glowed with an otherworldly light. The statue spoke, its voice deep and rumbling like thunder. "Only those who possess true courage may pass," it said. "Prove your heart is pure, and you shall be allowed to continue."

Amina, without hesitation, knelt before the statue. "I seek nothing for myself," she said, "only the chance to help my people. Please, let me pass."

The lion's eyes softened, and with a great roar, it stepped aside, allowing Amina to continue her journey. She smiled, grateful for the first step of her adventure.

✛ ✛ ✛

The path grew steeper as Amina climbed higher into the mountain, and soon she found herself facing a vast chasm, the distance across it too far to leap. But in the distance, she saw a beautiful golden rope hanging from the cliffs, swaying gently in the wind. This, too, was said to be part of the mountain's magic, and only the most deserving could use it.

Amina reached out, and to her surprise, the rope extended toward her, as though it recognized her presence. She grasped it firmly and climbed across the chasm with ease, the golden rope guiding her safely to the other side.

As she neared the summit, the air grew thin and the wind howled around her, as though the mountain itself was testing her resolve. Amina's strength began to waver, but then she heard a soft voice, the voice of the Mountain Spirit itself.

"You have proven yourself worthy, Amina," the Spirit said. "But there is one final trial. You must make your wish, but it must be one that will bring light to the world, not darkness."

Amina stood at the peak of Ntringui, gazing out over the land of Anjouan below. The village, with its struggling people, seemed so distant, and yet so close in her heart. She thought of her family, her friends, and all those she had left behind to climb the mountain.

Without hesitation, Amina closed her eyes and made her wish. "I wish for my people to have the strength to overcome their hardships, to live in harmony with the land, and to find prosperity in their hearts, not in riches, but in the love they share for one another."

The Mountain Spirit was silent for a moment, and then a great wind swept across the peak, lifting Amina's hair and filling her heart with warmth. The Spirit spoke softly, "Your wish is pure, Amina, and your heart is worthy. I shall grant it."

✢ ✢ ✢

As the wind faded, Amina saw something miraculous. From the peak of Ntringui, a golden light spread across the land, touching every corner of Anjouan. The rivers began to flow with abundance, the crops flourished, and the people found new strength and unity. The mountain had shared its magic with the world below, and Amina's wish had come true.

Amina returned to her village, not with riches, but with a heart full of joy. She shared her tale with the people, and they, too, felt the mountain's magic within them. The village thrived, not because of gold, but because of the love and unity that blossomed in their hearts.

And so, the Mountain Ntringui remained a place of wonder, a symbol of the power of a pure heart and the magic of selfless love. It stood as a reminder to all who sought its peak: that true wealth is not found in gold or jewels, but in the kindness we share with the world and the strength we find within ourselves.

Amina grew into a wise and beloved leader, her story inspiring generations to come. And though she never climbed Ntringui again, she often stood at the foot of the mountain, gazing up at its majestic peak, knowing that its magic lived on—not just in the land, but in the hearts of her people.

For in the heart of Anjouan, the spirit of Ntringui endures, a beacon of hope, unity, and the enduring power of a wish made with love.

THE BARREN WOMAN AND THE VISION OF THE STRONG MAN

*I*n a small village resting at the edge of a sprawling desert, there lived a kind-hearted woman named Fatima. She had been married to Omar, the love of her life, for fifteen years. Their home was filled with warmth, laughter, and a deep bond of love, but one thing was missing—a child.

Fatima's heart ached with longing as she watched the neighborhood children run and laugh, their mothers calling after them with smiles. She had prayed countless times, hoping for the day her home would echo with the laughter of her own child. Though the villagers sympathized with her, offering kind words and understanding looks, it was hard to quiet the deep sadness she carried inside. Each passing year only made the silence in her home feel heavier, and every giggle she heard in the distance was a bittersweet reminder of what she yearned for most.

Fatima and Omar had tried everything: consulting healers, making offerings, praying to the gods, but nothing seemed to change. The years passed, and though their love for each other grew stronger, the void of childlessness remained a heavy burden.

✦ ✦ ✦

One quiet night, as the moon hung high in the sky, Fatima fell into a deep sleep. As she drifted into dreams, something extraordinary happened. In her dream, a powerful figure appeared before her — a man of great strength, his body glowing with an aura of light. His eyes shone like the sun, and his voice was deep, resonating with an ancient power.

"Fatima," the strong man spoke, his words echoing in her dream. "I know the sorrow in your heart, and I offer you a choice. If you wish to have children, you may choose to give birth every year. But know this: each child will live for only fifteen years. They will grow quickly, and then they will leave this world, one after another."

Fatima's heart wrenched at the thought of losing her children so young, yet the possibility of being a mother, even if briefly, was a tempting thought.

The man continued, "Or, you may choose to wait for fifteen years. If you choose this path, you will bear a child who will grow into a mighty ruler, a king whose reign will be long and prosperous. But you must wait for the full fifteen years before this child is born."

Fatima was stunned. The decision seemed impossible—would she choose the fleeting joy of motherhood, knowing the pain of loss, or would she endure the long wait for a child destined for greatness?

She lay there in the dream, torn by her emotions. But then, something shifted in her heart. Fatima thought of her husband, Omar, and how they had always dreamed of having a child who would one day bring honor to their family and their people. She thought of the joy they would feel to watch that child grow into a wise and compassionate ruler.

With resolve, Fatima made her choice. "I choose to wait," she said, her voice strong with conviction. "I will wait for fifteen years to bear a child who will become a king."

The strong man smiled, his face filled with approval. "You have made a wise choice, Fatima. The path will be long, but in the end, your sacrifice will bring forth a legacy that will endure for generations. May your heart be steadfast, for the wait is not easy, but the reward will be great."

With that, the dream faded, and Fatima awoke in her bed, the morning sun shining through the window. She felt a deep sense of peace within her, knowing that she had made the right choice.

The next fifteen years were long and filled with moments of doubt and longing. Fatima and Omar endured the passage of time with patience and perseverance. Every day, Fatima would remind herself of the promise she had made in her dream. She tended to her garden, cared for her home, and supported her husband, all while keeping her faith that the child she had waited for was still to come.

The years were not without their challenges. Fatima grew older, and sometimes she wondered if she had made the right choice. But she held firm to the vision of the future — a child who would be a king, wise and noble. She trusted that the dream she had was a promise, and she believed that the waiting would be worth it.

Then, as the fifteenth year approached, something miraculous happened. Fatima discovered that she was with child. Her heart leapt with joy, for she knew that this was the fulfillment of her dream. She and Omar rejoiced, and the whole village celebrated with them.

Months passed, and Fatima gave birth to a healthy, strong boy. They named him Idris, and as he grew, it became clear that he was unlike any child the village had ever seen. From an early age, Idris displayed remarkable intelligence and a natural sense of leadership. He was wise beyond his years, and even as a young boy, he could command the respect of the village elders. His kindness and compassion were evident in every action he took, and soon it became known that he was destined for greatness.

When Idris reached the age of fifteen, the people of the village looked on in awe. He had grown into a young man, wise and capable, with a strong sense of justice and an unwavering heart. His leadership skills surpassed those of many seasoned rulers, and he quickly became a beloved figure in the region.

True to the dream that Fatima had been given all those years ago, Idris ascended to the throne as the king of the village. His reign was long and prosperous, marked by peace, wisdom, and prosperity. Under his rule, the people flourished, and his name became known far and wide as a just and fair ruler who cared deeply for the well-being of his people.

⚜ ⚜ ⚜

As for Fatima and Omar, they lived to see their son become the king they had always dreamed of. Their hearts were full of pride and joy, knowing that their sacrifice had brought forth a legacy that would live on for generations.

Fatima often reflected on the choice she had made all those years ago. She knew that the path she had chosen had not been easy, but it had been the right one. Her patience and faith had been rewarded, not just with a son, but with a king whose reign would bring light and prosperity to the world.

And so, the tale of Fatima and the vision of the strong man became a legend, passed down through generations as a reminder of the power of patience, faith, and the enduring strength of a mother's love.

In the quiet moments of her life, Fatima would sit by the window, gazing out at the desert and the village that had flourished under her son's rule. She would smile, knowing that her choice had not only fulfilled her own heart's desire but had also brought hope and prosperity to her people.

For in the heart of the desert, the legacy of Fatima and Idris endured, a testament to the power of sacrifice, the strength of faith, and the enduring light of a mother's love.

THE POOR MAN OF MBADJINI AND THE SECRET TREASURE

*O*nce upon a time, in the remote region of Mbadjini, there lived a poor man named M'madi. He was a humble man, living in a small, modest hut at the edge of the village. Though his heart was kind, M'madi's life was one of hardship and struggle. His clothes were worn, his shoes tattered, and his stomach often empty. The other villagers, who were wealthier and more prosperous, would mock and laugh at him. They called him "the poor fool" and often made fun of his misfortune.

Despite their ridicule, M'madi remained gentle and always tried to help others whenever he could. His days were spent in the fields, working tirelessly, and his evenings were spent collecting firewood and searching for what little food he could find in the nearby forest. He never complained, for he had learned to live with the hand life had dealt him.

+ + +

One day, after a long day of work in the fields, M'madi took his panga — his only tool — and went into the forest to collect firewood. He wandered deeper into the forest than usual, gathering branches and twigs, his heart content with the simple task. The sun began to set, casting a golden light through the trees, and as he made his way back to his hut, M'madi realized something troubling: he had forgotten his panga in the forest.

M'madi sighed, but he had no choice. The forest was vast, and returning for his panga in the dark would be dangerous. So, he decided to sleep through the night and return for it the next day. He walked back to his humble home, ate a small meal, and went to bed, exhausted from the day's labor.

That night, as he lay asleep, something extraordinary happened. M'madi dreamed a strange dream. In the dream, he found himself standing in the forest, near the very spot where he had left his panga the day before. A mysterious figure appeared before him — a wise old man, cloaked in a robe that shimmered with an ethereal light.

The old man spoke, his voice gentle yet commanding. "M'madi, I have seen your struggles and your heart. You are kind, and your patience is great, but your fate has been shaped by your poverty. You have been mocked and laughed at, yet you remain humble. Tonight, I offer you a choice, for the forest holds a secret beneath your feet."

M'madi listened attentively, his heart racing. The old man continued, "If you seek to find your panga, know that it is not the tool you have left behind, but something far more valuable. Where you find your panga, you must dig. Beneath the earth, there lies great wealth, hidden for those with pure hearts. But you must dig with care, for greed can turn even the purest of hearts to stone."

M'madi's eyes widened in disbelief. "But I am just a poor man," he said. "How can I find such wealth? And how can I be sure that it will not lead to more suffering?"

The old man smiled kindly. "The wealth you will find is not gold or jewels, but a blessing that will transform your life. Dig, and you will see. But remember, the true wealth lies in what you do with it."

With that, the old man vanished, leaving M'madi alone in the forest. As he awoke from the dream, the first light of dawn broke through the window, and M'madi felt a strange sense of purpose. He had never been one to seek fortune, but the dream had filled him with a sense of hope and curiosity.

✛ ✛ ✛

That morning, M'madi set out once again for the forest. He retraced his steps from the previous day, and as he reached the spot where he had left his panga, he began to dig as the old man had instructed. At first, the earth was hard, but as M'madi dug deeper, the ground softened, and his shovel hit something solid.

With great effort, M'madi cleared the earth around the object. As he lifted it, he was stunned to find an ancient chest, worn by time but still intact. His heart raced as he opened the chest, and inside, he discovered not gold or jewels, but a collection of rare and precious seeds — seeds that shimmered with an otherworldly glow.

M'madi could scarcely believe his eyes. These were not ordinary seeds. He had heard legends of such seeds — seeds that could grow into trees bearing fruits of unimaginable abundance, providing nourishment and wealth to those who knew how to cultivate them. It was said that these trees could heal the sick, purify the land, and bring prosperity to entire villages.

With great care, M'madi gathered the seeds and returned to his village. He knew that his life would never be the same, for he now held in his hands the key to a future far brighter than he had ever dreamed.

╬ ╬ ╬

In the following weeks, M'madi planted the seeds in his fields. As the trees grew, they flourished with remarkable speed. The fruits they bore were unlike anything anyone had ever seen. They were sweet and nourishing, and they healed the sick. The village, which had once laughed at

M'madi, now came to him in awe, begging for a share of the miraculous bounty.

But M'madi, with his kind heart, did not hoard the fruits for himself. He shared them with the people, helping them to plant their own trees, teaching them the art of cultivation and the lessons of generosity. Soon, the entire village thrived, and M'madi was no longer the poor man who had been mocked. He became a symbol of wisdom and compassion, beloved by all.

✛ ✛ ✛

As the years passed, M'madi's humble farm grew into a prosperous estate, and the wealth he had uncovered in the forest spread throughout the village. The villagers, who had once laughed at him, now came to him for guidance, and he became a wise leader, helping others to find the same prosperity and peace that he had found.

M'madi often reflected on the dream that had changed his life. He knew that the true treasure was not the seeds themselves, but the lessons they had taught him — the importance of kindness, generosity, and the power of sharing one's blessings with others.

And so, M'madi's life was transformed — not by gold or jewels, but by the hidden wealth beneath the earth, a wealth that brought prosperity to his people and healing to the land. He had learned that true wealth was not in the material riches that one could possess, but in the kindness, generosity, and wisdom one shared with others.

From that day on, M'madi lived a life of happiness and fulfillment, and the villagers of Mbadjini never mocked him again. Instead, they came to him with respect and gratitude, knowing that the poor man who had once been ridiculed had become the greatest treasure their village had ever known.

The tale of M'madi and the secret treasure became a legend, passed down through generations as a reminder of the power of humility, generosity, and the enduring strength of a pure heart. And in the quiet moments of his life, M'madi would sit beneath the shade of the miraculous trees, gazing out at the thriving village, knowing that his greatest treasure was not the wealth he had found, but the love and respect he had earned.

For in the heart of Mbadjini, the legacy of M'madi endured, a testament to the power of kindness, the strength of faith, and the enduring light of a humble heart.

THE MAN FROM MOHÉLI AND THE MERMAID'S ENCHANTMENT

*O*nce upon a time, on the lush island of Mohéli in the Comoros, there lived a young fisherman named Kamil. His life was simple yet content; he spent his days on the sparkling seas, casting his nets and bringing in the freshest catch for his village. The people of Mohéli knew him as a kind-hearted and hard-working soul, and though he lived humbly, he was well-loved by all.

Kamil's days began with the rising sun, as he set out in his small wooden boat, the waves lapping gently against its sides. He loved the sea—its vastness, its mysteries, and the way it provided for his village. But deep down, Kamil often felt a longing for something more, something he couldn't quite name.

+ + +

One evening, after a long day at sea, Kamil went to the shore to clean his boat. The sun was setting, casting a golden glow over the waves. As he worked, he heard a soft, melodic song carried by the wind. He turned his head, puzzled by the beautiful sound, and saw a figure perched on a large rock near the water's edge.

It was a woman, but unlike any woman Kamil had ever seen. Her long, flowing hair shimmered like the ocean, and her skin glistened as though it had been kissed by the sea itself. Below her waist, instead of legs, she had a shimmering fish's tail. Kamil gasped, for he had never heard of such a creature. She was a mermaid, a mystical being of the sea.

The mermaid's eyes, the color of the deep ocean, met Kamil's, and a spark of connection ignited between them. She smiled, her voice soft and enchanting, "Do not be afraid, young fisherman. I have been watching you for some time. Your heart is pure, and you are kind to the ocean."

Kamil, entranced by her beauty and the gentleness of her voice, stepped closer. "Who are you?" he asked, his voice trembling with wonder.

"I am Yara," she replied, "a mermaid of the sea. I have lived beneath these waters for many years, but I long for a love that transcends the waves."

Kamil's heart fluttered as he looked into Yara's eyes. In that moment, he knew that he had fallen in love with her. Despite the impossibility of their love, something deep inside him told him that he could not let this connection slip away.

+ + +

Over the next few days, Kamil returned to the same spot on the shore, where Yara would wait for him. They spoke of their dreams, of the world above and below the water, and of the love that blossomed between them. Each day, their bond grew stronger, and soon, they could no longer imagine life without each other.

But the villagers of Mohéli did not understand. When they saw Kamil spending more and more time at the water's edge, they grew suspicious. One day, they followed him and discovered the truth of his secret love for Yara. The villagers were outraged.

"How can you love a creature of the sea?" they demanded. "She is not one of us! She is a danger to our way of life!"

The village elders gathered to discuss the matter, and their verdict was harsh. They declared that Kamil must sever ties with Yara and never return to the shore where she lived. If he disobeyed, they warned, the seas would become angry and their village would be cursed.

Kamil's heart was torn. He loved Yara more than anything, but the pressure of the villagers' condemnation weighed heavily on him. His family begged him to forget the mermaid, telling him that it was unnatural and foolish to pursue such a love. Yet, the more they tried to convince him, the more Kamil knew that his heart belonged to Yara, and that no amount of scorn could change his feelings.

+ + +

One moonlit night, when the stars were bright above and the sea was calm, Kamil went to the shore one last time. Yara was waiting for him, her eyes filled with sadness.

"I cannot stay away from you, Kamil," Yara said softly. "But if we continue this love, the villagers will never accept us. They will try to separate us forever."

Kamil, his voice filled with determination, replied, "I do not care what they say. My heart is yours, and no one can take that away from us. We are meant to be together, no matter the cost."

With a sorrowful smile, Yara reached out her hand to Kamil. "Then, come with me. We can leave the land behind and live together beneath the waves. The sea is vast, and there is a place for us both. In my world, no one will judge our love."

Kamil hesitated, looking back at the village one last time. He thought of his family, his friends, and the life he had known. But then he looked into Yara's eyes, and all doubt disappeared. He knew that he could not live without her.

Without another word, Kamil stepped into the water, and Yara took his hand. As they dove deep into the ocean, the waters embraced them, and Kamil felt his body change. His legs fused together, becoming a tail like Yara's, and he found himself able to breathe underwater as though it was his natural home.

They swam together, hand in hand, deeper and deeper into the heart of the ocean. The coral reefs sparkled like jewels, and the sea creatures welcomed them as they journeyed to a hidden kingdom beneath the waves. There, in the tranquility of the deep, Kamil and Yara built a life together, free from the judgment of the land above.

Yara showed Kamil the wonders of the underwater world — the vibrant coral gardens, the schools of fish that danced like rainbows, and the ancient ruins of a forgotten civilization. Kamil, in turn, shared stories of the land above, of the sunsets and the laughter of children. Together, they created a life that was a perfect blend of both worlds.

Years passed, and the village of Mohéli began to forget the tale of the fisherman who had fallen in love with a mermaid. But sometimes, on moonlit nights, the villagers would hear a soft, melodic song carried on the wind, and they would remember the love that had once defied the waves.

Kamil and Yara, now rulers of the underwater kingdom, were happy. They had found their peace in the sea, where love knew no boundaries. And though the world above them could never understand, their hearts were one, and that was all that mattered.

✦ ✦ ✦

And so, the love between Kamil and Yara became a legend of the sea, a tale of love so strong that it could not be held by the shores of the land. For in the depths of the ocean, true love is eternal.

The villagers of Mohéli, though they had once scorned Kamil's love, came to see it as a reminder of the power of love and the importance of following one's heart. They told the story to their children, who told it to theirs, and the legend of Kamil and Yara lived on, a testament to the enduring strength of love that transcends all boundaries.

And in the quiet moments of the night, when the waves whispered their secrets, the people of Mohéli would look out at the sea and remember the fisherman and the mermaid, whose love had become a beacon of hope and a reminder that true love knows no limits.

THE MAN WHO DARED TO DEFY GOD

*O*nce upon a time, in a small village nestled between towering mountains, there lived a man named Ismail. Ismail was not just any man—he was a force of nature. His strength was unmatched, his wit razor-sharp, and his confidence unshakable. He was the kind of man who could lift a boulder with one hand, outsmart the cleverest of foxes, and win any competition the village threw his way. But Ismail's greatest strength was also his greatest weakness: his pride.

Ismail believed he was invincible. He often boasted to the villagers, "There is nothing I cannot do, no challenge I cannot overcome. I am stronger, smarter, and braver than anyone—even God Himself!" The villagers, who were simple and devout, would shake their heads and warn him, "Ismail, pride is a dangerous thing. Even the mightiest tree can be felled by a single storm." But Ismail would just laugh, his voice echoing through the valley. "Let the storm come! I will stand tall!"

The villagers admired Ismail's strength and courage, but they also feared his arrogance. They knew that pride, like a wildfire, could consume everything in its path.

+ + +

One day, after winning yet another village contest—this time a wrestling match against three men at once—Ismail climbed to the highest hill overlooking the village. The sun was setting, casting a golden glow over the mountains. He raised his arms to the heavens and shouted, "I am the greatest of all! I challenge anyone—even God—to prove me wrong! Let us see who is truly the mightiest!"

The villagers gasped. The wind seemed to still, and the birds fell silent. Even the elders, who had seen many things in their long lives, were struck with fear. "Ismail," one of them called out, "do not tempt fate. Humility is the path to wisdom." But Ismail only smirked. "Wisdom? I don't need wisdom. I have strength!"

Unbeknownst to Ismail, his challenge had not gone unheard. Far above, in the realm beyond time and space, God listened. And God, in His infinite wisdom, decided to teach Ismail a lesson—not out of anger, but out of love. For God knew that true strength lies not in the body, but in the heart and mind.

+ + +

The next morning, as Ismail stood in the village square boasting of his victory, a figure appeared before him. It was not a figure of wrath or thunder, but of light and peace. The villagers fell to their knees, but Ismail stood tall, though his heart raced.

"Ismail," God said, His voice both gentle and commanding, "you have challenged Me. Very well. I will give you three tasks. If you succeed, you will prove your strength. But if you fail, you will learn the true meaning of power."

God pointed to a distant mountain, its peak shrouded in clouds. "Your first task is to climb that mountain and bring Me the rare flower that blooms only at its summit. The journey will test your strength, but also your patience and perseverance."

Ismail laughed. "A simple climb? I could do that in my sleep!" Without another word, he set off.

The journey was grueling. The forest was thick with thorns, the rivers swift and cold. Ismail's muscles ached, but his pride pushed him forward. After days of struggle, he reached the summit. There, bathed in sunlight, was the flower—a single, radiant bloom. Ismail plucked it triumphantly and began his descent.

But as he climbed down, the flower grew heavier in his hand. The path, which had seemed clear before, became treacherous. His legs trembled, and he stumbled, falling to his knees. Exhausted, he cried out, "Why is this so hard? I am strong! I should be able to do this!"

God's voice echoed in the wind. "Ismail, strength alone is not enough. The mountain teaches patience, perseverance, and humility. You cannot conquer it with pride."

Ismail, humbled, whispered, "I see now. I was wrong."

✦ ✦ ✦

For his second task, God led Ismail to a vast desert. The sun blazed overhead, and the sand stretched endlessly in every direction. "Cross this desert," God said. "Find the oasis at its farthest point. But remember, the journey will test not only your endurance but also your understanding."

Ismail set out, his confidence renewed. But the desert was merciless. The sun scorched his skin, and the sand burned his feet. Days passed, and his water ran out. His throat was parched, and his vision blurred. Just as he was about to collapse, he saw it—a shimmering oasis. He stumbled toward it, his heart racing. But as he reached out to touch the water, it vanished.

"A mirage," he whispered, falling to his knees.

God's voice came again. "Ismail, you rushed forward without understanding. True strength lies in patience and wisdom. Sometimes, the oasis is not where you expect it to be."

Ismail bowed his head. "I understand now. I was too hasty, too proud."

For his final task, God led Ismail to a vast ocean. The waves crashed against the shore, and the wind howled. "Build a boat," God said, "and sail across this ocean. But remember, your boat must be built not only of strength but also of humility."

Ismail worked tirelessly, crafting a boat from the strongest wood he could find. He was determined to prove himself. But as he sailed into the ocean, a storm arose. The waves grew fierce, and the wind tore at his sails. His boat, built with pride and strength alone, began to crack.

"No!" Ismail cried, trying to hold the boat together. But it was no use. The boat sank, and he was left adrift in the cold, dark water.

God's voice carried over the waves. "Ismail, you cannot conquer the storm with strength alone. Life's challenges require wisdom, humility, and trust in something greater than yourself."

Exhausted and humbled, Ismail floated in the water, his pride washed away by the waves. God appeared before him, His light warm and comforting. "Ismail," He said, "you have learned the greatest lesson of all: true strength lies in humility, wisdom, and understanding. I grant you this gift — use it well."

Ismail returned to his village a changed man. He no longer boasted of his strength or challenged the heavens. Instead, he became a wise and humble leader, guiding others with the lessons he had learned.

And so, the man who once dared to defy God became a beacon of wisdom, proving that true greatness is not found in pride, but in the quiet strength of a humble heart.

THE WICKED WITCH AND THE BABY WHO OVERCAME HER

Once upon a time, in a quiet village nestled in a lush green valley surrounded by dense forests, life was simple but fraught with fear. The villagers lived under the shadow of a wicked witch who dwelled in a dark cave deep within the woods. For as long as anyone could remember, she had terrorized the village with her dark powers. Crops withered under her curses, sickness spread through her malice, and worst of all, she had a horrifying tradition—she would steal every newborn baby born in the village.

No one knew why she did it. Some said she was cursed herself, others believed she fed on the sorrow of others, and a few whispered that she was once a mother who had lost her own child and now sought to destroy the joy she could never have. Whatever the reason, the villagers lived in despair, their hearts heavy with grief and fear.

The villagers tried everything to stop her. They built stronger doors, set traps, and even sought the help of wandering priests and wise women, but nothing worked. The witch always came, her eyes glowing like embers, her long, bony fingers curling like claws. She would slip into homes under the cover of night, snatch the babies from their cradles, and cast a dreadful spell that sent them into an eternal sleep. The village was cursed, and no joy could last.

But then, one fateful day, hope was born.

Alim and Nadia, a kind and hardworking couple who had longed for a child for many years, welcomed a baby boy into the world. They named him Samir, which meant "companion in evening conversation," for they hoped he would bring light to their darkest hours. Samir was a small, delicate child with bright, curious eyes and a smile that seemed to radiate warmth. His laughter was like music, and his presence filled the hearts of his parents and the villagers with a joy they had almost forgotten.

The villagers celebrated Samir's birth, but their joy was tinged with fear. They knew the witch would come for him, as she had come for all the others. Alim and Nadia, determined to protect their child, kept watch over him day and night. They lit candles in every corner of their home, hung charms above his cradle, and prayed fervently for his safety.

That night, as the full moon cast an eerie glow over the village, the witch emerged from her cave. She moved silently through the forest, her tattered robes brushing against the trees, her eyes glowing with malice. She had heard of the baby's birth, and her heart burned with envy. She could not allow such a pure soul to live.

When she reached Alim and Nadia's humble home, she peered through the window and saw Samir sleeping peacefully in his cradle. For a moment, she hesitated. The baby's face was so innocent, so full of light, that it stirred something deep within her—a memory, perhaps, of a time long ago when she herself had known love. But the moment passed, and her wicked nature took over. She raised her bony fingers to cast her dark spell.

Just as she began to chant, Samir's eyes fluttered open. Instead of crying or screaming, as the witch expected, he smiled—a bright, radiant smile that seemed to light up the room. The witch froze, her incantation faltering. She had never seen a baby look at her with such warmth and fearlessness.

Samir's smile grew wider, and a soft, glowing light began to emanate from him. It was not just the light of innocence; it was something far more powerful. It was the pure, untainted love that radiated from his tiny heart, a force so strong that it pushed against the witch's dark magic.

The witch stumbled back, her eyes wide with shock. She tried to continue her spell, but the words caught in her throat. The light grew brighter, filling the room and spilling out into the night. It was as if Samir's very soul was fighting back, not with anger or hatred, but with love and joy.

The witch screamed as the light burned her, her dark powers crumbling like ash in the wind. She tried to retreat, but the light followed her, pushing her back toward the forest. The more she struggled, the weaker she became, until finally, with a howl of defeat, she vanished into the shadows, never to be seen again.

When dawn broke, the villagers awoke to the sound of Samir's laughter. Word spread quickly that the witch had been defeated, and it was the baby who had done it. The villagers rushed to Alim and Nadia's home, their hearts filled with gratitude and wonder. They marveled at how a child, so small and innocent, had destroyed the evil that had plagued their lives for generations.

As the years passed, Samir grew into a young man, wise beyond his years. His light-hearted nature never dimmed, and the village prospered under his care. He became a protector of his people, not through force, but through love, understanding, and the purity of heart that had once defeated the witch.

Alim and Nadia lived to see their son grow into a strong, compassionate leader. They often told him the story of how he had saved the village, not to boast, but to remind him of the power of love and goodness. Samir, in turn, shared the story with others, teaching them that even in the face of great evil, the light within us could overcome any darkness.

The tale of Samir, the boy who had defeated the wicked witch, became a legend, passed down from generation to generation. It was a story of hope, of the triumph of love over hatred, and of the enduring power of innocence. And though the village had endured much sorrow in the past, they now knew peace, for Samir's love had brought a light that no darkness could ever overcome.

Years later, on the edge of the forest, a small flower bloomed where the witch had vanished. It was a rare and beautiful flower, its petals glowing softly in the moonlight. The villagers believed it was a sign that even the darkest hearts could find redemption, and they tended to it with care.

Samir, now an old man, would often visit the flower with his grandchildren. He would tell them the story of the wicked witch and the baby who had overcome her, reminding them that love and kindness were the greatest powers in the world. And as the children listened, their eyes wide with wonder, they knew that the light of Samir's heart would live on forever.

THE MOSQUE THAT WOKE MBADJINI

L ong ago, in the serene and picturesque land of Mbadjini, a small village nestled between rolling green hills and the shimmering blue sea, life was simple but deeply spiritual. The villagers were kind-hearted, hardworking, and devout, but they lacked a central place to gather and worship. Each family prayed in their own homes, yearning for a space where they could come together as one community to honor their faith.

Among the villagers was Ali, a humble farmer known for his gentle heart and unwavering devotion. Though he had little in the way of material wealth, Ali was rich in spirit and generosity. He often shared what little he had with others, whether it was a basket of fruit from his orchard or a kind word of encouragement. One evening, as he sat outside his modest home, gazing at the stars, a thought struck him: *Our village needs a mosque — a house of prayer where we can gather, support one another, and strengthen our faith.*

From that night on, Ali made it his mission to build a mosque. After long days tending to his fields, he would walk to the riverbank to collect stones and clay, carrying them back to a small plot of land he had chosen for the mosque. With his own hands, he began shaping the walls, brick by brick, under the light of the moon.

The work was slow and grueling, and progress was hard to see. Months turned into years, and the mosque remained incomplete. Some villagers, seeing Ali's tireless efforts, shook their heads in pity. "Ali," they would say, "why do you keep working on this? You'll never finish it alone. It's too much for one man." But Ali would simply smile and reply, "Even if I don't finish, perhaps my efforts will inspire someone else to continue. A mosque is not just a building; it's a dream for our community."

Despite his determination, there were moments when Ali felt the weight of his task. One cool, starry night, as he sat by the half-built mosque, his hands calloused and his body weary, he whispered a prayer: "Oh Allah, bless this village with a house of worship. Let it be a light for all of us, a place where we can come together in Your name." With that, he laid down on the cool earth and drifted into a deep, dreamless sleep.

The next morning, Ali woke to the sound of excited voices. He sat up, rubbing his eyes, and gasped at the sight before him. Where the unfinished walls had stood the night before, a majestic mosque now towered, its walls gleaming like polished pearls and its golden dome catching the first rays of the morning sun. The villagers had gathered, their faces filled with awe and wonder.

"Ali, did you see this? It's a miracle!" someone shouted. Ali, tears streaming down his face, fell to his knees. "This is not my work," he whispered. "This is a gift from Allah, a blessing for our village."

They named it *The Miracle Mosque*, but the miracles didn't stop there. Each morning at dawn, a beautiful, melodic call to prayer echoed from the mosque, though no one stood in the minaret. The sound was unlike anything the villagers had ever heard—gentle yet powerful, stirring their hearts and drawing them from their homes to gather and pray. Those who entered the mosque felt an unexplainable peace, as though their burdens were being lifted and their spirits renewed.

Word of the mosque spread far and wide, reaching distant islands and bustling cities. Travelers began arriving in Mbadjini, eager to see the mosque for themselves. One such traveler, an elderly man with a long white beard and kind eyes, stepped inside and immediately felt tears welling up. "This is no ordinary place," he said to the villagers. "There is something divine here. I can feel it in my soul."

The villagers gathered around him, eager to hear his thoughts. The traveler shared an old legend he had heard as a child—a tale about a mosque that would build itself for a people pure of heart, guided by the prayers of the faithful. "This must be the one," he said with conviction. "Your village has been blessed because of your unity, your faith, and the selflessness of one man who dared to dream."

From that day on, the mosque became more than just a place of prayer. It was a symbol of unity, hope, and the power of faith. The villagers took great care to maintain the mosque, ensuring it remained a beacon of light for generations to come. They planted gardens around it, filled with fragrant flowers and fruit trees, and built a small school nearby where children could learn about their faith and heritage.

Ali, though he never sought recognition, became a beloved figure in the village. His story inspired others to give selflessly and to believe in the power of dreams. He often reminded the villagers, "The mosque is not just a building; it is a reminder of what we can achieve when we come together with faith and love."

Years passed, and the Miracle Mosque continued to stand tall and proud, its golden dome shining like a beacon over Mbadjini. The melodic call to prayer still echoed each morning, awakening the villagers not just from their sleep, but to the beauty of their shared faith and community.

And so, the mosque that woke Mbadjini became a living testament to the magic that can happen when faith, hard work, and hope come together. It was a reminder that even the smallest acts of devotion can lead to miracles, and that the purest hearts can move the heavens.

Generations later, the story of Ali and the Miracle Mosque was passed down from parents to children, becoming a cherished part of Mbadjini's history. The mosque remained a place of peace and inspiration, drawing people from all walks of life who sought solace and connection.

One day, a young girl named Amina, the great-granddaughter of Ali, stood in the mosque's courtyard, gazing up at the golden dome. She turned to her father and asked, "Do you think Ali ever imagined his dream would last this long?"

Her father smiled and placed a hand on her shoulder. "Ali didn't dream for himself," he said. "He dreamed for all of us. And as long as we keep his spirit alive, the mosque will always be a light for Mbadjini."

Amina nodded, her heart swelling with pride. She knew then that she, too, would carry on Ali's legacy—not just by caring for the mosque, but by living a life of faith, kindness, and unwavering hope.

And so, the Miracle Mosque continued to stand, not just as a place of worship, but as a living reminder of the power of one man's dream and the strength of a community united in faith.

THE TALE OF THE SHADOW WARRIOR AND THE ISLES OF PEACE

*O*nce upon a time, in the crystal-blue waters of the Indian Ocean, there lay a cluster of enchanting islands known as the Isles of Peace. These islands, adorned with lush greenery, golden sands, and swaying palm trees, were home to a proud and harmonious people. The islanders lived simply but richly, their lives intertwined with the rhythms of the sea and the land. They fished in the turquoise waters, cultivated fragrant spices in their fertile soil, and gathered under the starlit skies to sing songs of brotherhood and gratitude.

The Isles of Peace were not just a place; they were a way of life. The people believed in the power of unity and the strength of their shared history. They were guided by three wise leaders: Ali of the Stars, a visionary who could read the heavens and predict the seasons; Ahmed of the Palms, a gentle soul who mediated disputes with kindness and wisdom; and Taki of the Horizon, a fearless protector who patrolled the shores to keep the islands safe. Together, they ensured that the Isles remained a haven of peace and prosperity.

But far across the seas, in a distant land of misty towers and cobblestone streets, a shadowy figure known as the Phantom of Winds plotted in the darkness. His name was Benoît the Wanderer, a man cloaked in mystery and whispered about in fear. Some called him a warrior, others a harbinger of storms. He was a master of deception, a weaver of chaos who thrived on sowing discord and bending the wills of others to his own.

One fateful day, the rulers of a powerful empire, envious of the Isles' tranquility and abundance, sought Benoît's cunning. They promised him riches and power in exchange for a dark deed: to infiltrate the Isles of Peace and fracture their unity, making them vulnerable to foreign control.

Benoît accepted the task without hesitation. Disguised as a humble trader, he arrived on the shores of the Isles, his ship laden with exotic goods and his silver tongue ready to spin tales. At first, the islanders welcomed him, for they were a trusting people. But Benoît's shadowy influence soon began to creep into their hearts.

He whispered lies into the ears of the ambitious, stoking their desires for power. He planted seeds of doubt among the fearful, convincing them that their neighbors could not be trusted. Slowly, the harmony of the Isles began to unravel. Leaders who had once stood as pillars of the community fell to mysterious misfortunes. Ali of the Stars was accused of hoarding knowledge, Ahmed of the Palms was blamed for favoring certain families, and Taki of the Horizon was framed for crimes he did not commit.

Without their guiding hands, the Isles trembled. The once harmonious songs of brotherhood grew faint, replaced by murmurs of doubt and sorrow. The people, once united, now turned against one another, their hearts heavy with mistrust.

But even in the darkest times, light can emerge.

Deep in the forests of the largest island, a young storyteller named Amina lived with her grandmother, the keeper of the island's oldest tales. Amina had always been fascinated by the stories of her ancestors—tales of courage, unity, and the power of forgiveness. One evening, as she wandered the forest, she stumbled upon a hidden cave where Benoît had been meeting with his conspirators. Hidden in the shadows, she overheard their plans and realized the truth: the Phantom of Winds was behind the chaos that had gripped her home.

Amina knew she had to act, but she had no weapons, no army, no power. All she had was her voice and the wisdom of her ancestors. She began to weave her own tales, stories that reminded the people of who they were and what they stood for. She spoke of Ali's selflessness, Ahmed's kindness, and Taki's bravery. She told of the times when the islanders had faced storms and invaders, and how they had always triumphed by standing together.

At first, her words were met with skepticism, but slowly, they began to take root. The people, weary of division and fear, started to remember the bonds that had once united them. They gathered in the village square to listen to Amina, her voice rising like a beacon of hope in the darkness.

One by one, the islanders began to see through Benoît's shadowy illusions. They realized that their strength lay not in division but in unity. Together, they confronted the Phantom of Winds, their hearts filled with courage and determination. Benoît, unprepared for their resolve, tried to escape, but the islanders stood firm, their unity unshakable.

In the end, Benoît was cast back into the seas, his schemes undone by the very people he had sought to destroy. The Isles of Peace began to heal, their songs of brotherhood echoing once more across the waves.

Amina, though young, became a symbol of hope and resilience. She continued to tell her stories, ensuring that the lessons of the past were never forgotten. The islanders rebuilt their lives, stronger and wiser than before, and the three leaders — Ali, Ahmed, and Taki — were honored as heroes who had sacrificed for the greater good.

Though the name Benoît faded into legend, the islanders never forgot the lesson he had taught them: that true strength lies not in division but in unity, and that even the darkest shadows can be dispelled by the light of a shared purpose.

Years later, Amina sat by the fire, surrounded by children eager to hear her tales. She smiled as she began the story of the Shadow Warrior and the Isles of Peace, her voice carrying the weight of history and the promise of hope.

"And so," she concluded, "we must always remember that our strength comes from standing together. For when we are united, no storm can break us, and no shadow can dim our light."

The children nodded, their eyes wide with wonder, and as they drifted off to sleep, the songs of the Isles of Peace echoed softly in the night, a reminder of the power of unity and the enduring spirit of a people who had chosen love over fear.

THE WISE MAN AND THE LOYAL FRIEND

*O*nce upon a time, in the quaint and picturesque village of Sima, nestled between rolling green hills and the endless blue sea, life was simple but rich in warmth and community. The villagers were known for their kindness and close-knit bonds, but among them, two friends stood out — Ali, the wise man, and Adi, his loyal companion.

Ali was a figure of great respect in Sima and beyond. His intelligence, compassion, and calm demeanor earned him admiration far and wide. He spent much of his time traveling to distant lands, learning from scholars, teaching those who sought knowledge, and gathering wisdom to bring back to his village. Yet, no matter how far he roamed, Ali always returned to Sima during the holidays, where his heart truly belonged.

Adi, on the other hand, was a simple man. He wasn't particularly wise or scholarly, but his heart was as vast as the ocean and as pure as the morning dew. He was a farmer who tended to his fields with care, and though his life was humble, he found joy in the little things—the laughter of children, the rustling of leaves, and the company of his dear friend Ali.

Whenever Ali returned to Sima, Adi would be the first to greet him, his face lighting up with a warm smile. He would prepare a feast from the best of what he could gather—freshly caught fish, ripe fruits from his orchard, and bread baked with his own hands. The two friends would sit under the ancient baobab tree at the edge of the village, sharing stories, laughing, and dreaming of the future.

"Adi," Ali would often say, "you are the anchor that keeps me grounded. No matter where I go, I always look forward to coming home to you."

Adi would grin and reply, "Ali, no matter how far you go, I will always be here for you. You're my brother, and that will never change."

Their bond was a source of joy for the entire village. The villagers often marveled at how two such different men could be so close. Ali, with his wisdom and worldly knowledge, and Adi, with his simplicity and boundless kindness, seemed to complement each other perfectly.

But life, as it often does, took an unexpected turn.

One year, Ali returned to Sima to find that Adi had changed. The villagers whispered among themselves, their voices tinged with pity and fear. Adi, they said, had lost his mind. He was seen speaking to the wind, laughing at the rain, and wandering the village at odd hours. Some avoided him, others mocked him, and a few even feared him.

Ali, however, saw only his old friend. While others turned their backs on Adi, Ali stood by him. He would sit beside Adi under the baobab tree, listening patiently to his ramblings, no matter how incoherent they seemed. When Adi wandered through the village, Ali made sure he was safe, guiding him gently back home. And when Adi seemed lost in his own world, Ali would remind him of their shared memories — the feasts they had shared, the stories they had told, the dreams they had dreamed.

In those moments, Adi's eyes would light up with recognition, and he would smile, a glimpse of the man he once was shining through.

The villagers were puzzled by Ali's unwavering loyalty. "Why do you care for him so much?" they asked. "He's no longer the friend you knew. He can't even hold a proper conversation anymore."

Ali would smile gently and reply, "Friendship is not about what someone can give you. It is about loyalty, love, and standing by each other, no matter the storm. Adi was there for me when I needed him, and I will be there for him now."

Years passed, and though Adi's mind never fully returned, his heart recognized Ali's unwavering support. Their friendship became a legend in Sima, a tale of devotion and loyalty that inspired everyone who heard it.

Even as they grew old, Ali and Adi could still be found under the baobab tree. Ali's hair had turned silver, and Adi's steps had grown slower, but their bond remained as strong as ever. The villagers no longer pitied Adi or questioned Ali's loyalty. Instead, they admired the two friends, seeing in them a reminder that true friendship endures all challenges.

One evening, as the sun dipped below the horizon, painting the sky in hues of orange and pink, Ali and Adi sat together under the baobab tree. Adi, in a rare moment of clarity, turned to Ali and said, "Thank you, my brother. You've always been my light."

Tears welled up in Ali's eyes as he clasped Adi's hand. "And you, Adi, have always been my anchor."

Their story lived on long after they were gone, passed down from generation to generation in Sima. It became a lesson in love, loyalty, and the enduring power of friendship. The villagers would point to the ancient baobab tree and tell their children, "That is where Ali and Adi sat, two friends who proved that love and loyalty can outshine even the darkest clouds."

And so, the tale of the wise man and his loyal friend remained a beacon of hope, reminding everyone that true friendship is not about perfection but about standing together, no matter what life may bring.

THE KING AND THE SERVANT: A TALE OF LOVE IN BIMBINI

*O*nce upon a time, on the lush and vibrant island of Anjouan, nestled in the Indian Ocean, there lay a picturesque village called Bimbini. The village was known for its rolling green hills, fragrant spice gardens, and the warm, welcoming spirit of its people. At the heart of Bimbini stood the royal palace, a grand structure of white stone and intricate carvings, where the young and noble King Abdul ruled with wisdom and fairness.

King Abdul was beloved by his people. He had inherited the throne at a young age and had spent his early years traveling the world, learning about different cultures, and bringing back knowledge to improve his kingdom. Despite his many achievements, there was one thing that eluded him — love. Though many noblewomen had sought his hand, none had captured his heart.

In the palace, among the many servants who worked tirelessly to maintain its splendor, was a young woman named Zahra. She was born into a family of humble means, her parents farmers who toiled in the fields to provide for their children. Zahra had grown up in poverty, but her spirit was unbroken. She was known for her radiant beauty, her laughter that could light up the darkest room, and her kind heart that touched everyone she met.

Zahra's days were filled with hard work — sweeping the palace halls, tending to the gardens, and serving meals to the royal family. Yet, she never complained. She found joy in the simple things: the scent of blooming flowers, the sound of the ocean waves, and the camaraderie of her fellow servants. Her kindness and humility made her a favorite among the palace staff, and her presence brought a sense of warmth to the grand, often cold, halls of the palace.

One fateful day, King Abdul returned from a long journey across the seas. As he walked through the palace gardens, he noticed Zahra kneeling in the soil, her hands gently planting flowers. The sunlight caught her face, and for a moment, the king was captivated. He had seen many beautiful women in his travels, but there was something about Zahra — her grace, her humility, the way she smiled as she worked — that stirred something deep within him.

From that day on, King Abdul found himself drawn to the gardens, where he would watch Zahra from a distance. He admired the way she treated everyone with kindness, from the youngest kitchen maid to the oldest gardener. He noticed how she always had a word of encouragement or a helping hand for those in need.

One evening, as the moon cast its silver light over the palace, King Abdul decided to approach Zahra. She was startled to see the king before her and immediately bowed, her hands trembling.

"Rise, Zahra," he said gently. "You need not bow before me. Your heart shines brighter than any crown I wear."

Zahra looked up, her eyes wide with surprise. She had never imagined that the king, a man of such stature, would speak to her. They began to talk, and as the nights passed, they shared stories of their lives. Zahra spoke of her struggles in Bimbini, her dreams of a better life for her family, and her love for the simple beauty of the island. Abdul shared his own challenges as a ruler, the weight of expectations, and the loneliness that came with his position.

Their bond grew stronger with each conversation, and soon, they realized they were in love. However, their love was not without challenges. The royal court was scandalized by the idea of a king falling in love with a servant. Whispers of disapproval echoed through the palace halls.

"She is not fit to be a queen," the advisors said. "A king must marry someone of noble birth."

But King Abdul would not be swayed. He stood before his advisors and declared, "A crown is not what makes one noble. It is the heart that matters. Zahra's heart is pure, and her love is true. She is fit to be queen because she embodies the virtues I wish to rule by—kindness, humility, and strength."

Despite the opposition, Abdul and Zahra were married in a grand ceremony in Bimbini. The village was adorned with flowers and lanterns, and the air was filled with music and laughter. Zahra's family and the villagers celebrated alongside the royal court, their hearts filled with joy and pride.

As queen, Zahra brought a new light to the palace. She used her position to help those in need, establishing schools for children, supporting farmers, and ensuring that no one in the kingdom went hungry. Her kindness and compassion endeared her to the people, and they soon embraced her as their queen.

Together, King Abdul and Queen Zahra ruled with wisdom and compassion, transforming the kingdom into a place where everyone, regardless of their background, had the chance to thrive. Their love story became a cherished legend, told by the people of Anjouan as a reminder that true love knows no boundaries.

✛ ✛ ✛

Years later, as King Abdul and Queen Zahra sat together in the palace gardens, watching their children play among the flowers, Zahra turned to Abdul and said, "Do you remember the day we first spoke under the moonlight?"

Abdul smiled and took her hand. "How could I forget? You were planting flowers, and I was captivated by your kindness. You've brought so much light to my life, Zahra."

Zahra leaned her head on his shoulder. "And you've given me a life I never dreamed possible. Together, we've built a kingdom where love and kindness reign."

Their love story continued to inspire generations, a testament to the power of love, humility, and the belief that true nobility lies in the heart. And so, the tale of the king and the servant became a beacon of hope, reminding everyone that love knows no boundaries and that even the humblest beginnings can lead to the greatest of destinies.

THE SELFISH KING AND THE FALL OF HIS KINGDOM

*O*nce upon a time, in a land of rolling hills, sparkling rivers, and golden fields, there lay the kingdom of Shissiwani. It was a place of abundance, where the air smelled of blooming flowers, the markets buzzed with laughter, and the people worked together to ensure everyone had enough. Shissiwani was not just a kingdom; it was a community, bound by shared labor and shared joy.

At the heart of this kingdom stood a grand palace, its towers reaching toward the heavens, its walls adorned with intricate carvings of the kingdom's history. Inside, however, the palace was cold and lifeless, a reflection of its ruler, King BA-Bacar.

King BA-Bacar was not always a selfish man. In his youth, he had been taught the virtues of leadership—compassion, fairness, and humility. But as the years passed, the weight of the crown and the whispers of power corrupted him. He began to see the kingdom not as a responsibility but as a possession, its people not as subjects to protect but as tools to exploit.

His greed grew like a weed, choking out the goodness in his heart. He demanded higher taxes, claiming it was for the kingdom's protection. He confiscated the best harvests, insisting the palace needed them more. He even closed the palace gates to the sick and hungry, declaring they were not his concern. While the people of Shissiwani toiled under the scorching sun, BA-Bacar dined on lavish feasts served on golden plates, his vaults overflowing with treasures he never used.

One day, an old farmer named Elias, his hands calloused and his back bent from years of labor, came to the palace gates. His face was etched with worry, his voice trembling as he spoke.

"Your Majesty," he pleaded, "a drought has destroyed our crops. My family has nothing to eat. Please, grant us some grain from your stores. We are not asking for much—just enough to survive."

King BA-Bacar, seated on his gilded throne, looked down at the farmer with disdain. "Why should I share what I have worked hard to take?" he sneered. "Your failures are not my concern. Be gone!"

Elias left the palace with a heavy heart, his hope shattered. Word of the king's cruelty spread quickly, carried by the whispers of the villagers. The people of Shissiwani, once proud and loyal, began to lose faith in their king. Farmers abandoned their fields, merchants closed their shops, and craftsmen packed their tools and sought refuge in neighboring lands. The kingdom, once vibrant and thriving, began to wither. The markets grew silent, the fields barren, and the streets empty.

Yet, despite the growing desolation, BA-Bacar remained blind to his folly. "Let them leave," he said, his voice dripping with arrogance. "I have my gold, and that is all I need."

One stormy night, as BA-Bacar sat alone in his treasure room, counting his gold by the flickering light of a candle, he heard a faint knock at the palace door. Annoyed, he stormed to the door and flung it open. Standing before him was an old woman, her face weathered by time, her eyes glowing with an otherworldly light. Her tattered robes hung loosely on her frail frame, and in her hand, she held a simple wooden staff.

"Who are you to disturb me?" BA-Bacar barked, his voice echoing through the empty halls.

"I am a messenger," the old woman replied, her voice calm but firm. "Your greed has destroyed not only your kingdom but your soul. If you do not change your ways, you will lose everything."

BA-Bacar laughed, a cold, hollow sound. "I have my wealth. That is all that matters."

The old woman's eyes narrowed, and for a moment, the air grew heavy with an unspoken warning. "Then so be it," she said. With a wave of her hand, she vanished into the night, leaving BA-Bacar standing alone in the darkness.

The next morning, BA-Bacar woke to find his treasure room empty. His gold, jewels, and precious artifacts had vanished without a trace. Panic surged through him as he searched every corner of the palace, but the riches were gone.

As days turned to weeks, the palace grew colder and more silent. Without his wealth, BA-Bacar found himself abandoned by his servants and advisors. The once-grand halls echoed with the sound of his footsteps, a haunting reminder of his isolation. Hungry and alone, he wandered the empty streets of Shissiwani, where the winds howled through the ruins of what had once been a bustling kingdom.

One day, as he sat by the dried-up fountain in the village square, a small child approached him. The child, no older than six, held a loaf of bread in their hands.

"Here, take this," the child said, offering the bread to BA-Bacar.

BA-Bacar, humbled and starving, accepted the bread with trembling hands. "Why would you help me?" he asked, his voice barely above a whisper.

The child smiled, their eyes filled with innocence and kindness. "Because kindness is what makes a kingdom strong, not gold."

In that moment, BA-Bacar felt a pang of regret so deep it brought tears to his eyes. He realized that his selfishness had not only ruined his kingdom but had also left him with nothing but emptiness.

Determined to change, BA-Bacar began working alongside the villagers, helping to rebuild what he had destroyed. He shared what little he had, tilled the fields, and repaired the crumbling homes. Though the work was hard, he found a sense of purpose he had never known before. Slowly, the people began to trust him again, not as a king but as a fellow human being.

Shissiwani, once on the brink of collapse, began to flourish once more. The fields turned green, the markets buzzed with life, and the laughter of children filled the air. BA-Bacar never regained his throne, but he earned something far more valuable: the trust and friendship of his people.

The story of the selfish king who became humble was told for generations, a reminder that true wealth lies not in gold or power but in the kindness and love we share with others. And so, Shissiwani became a beacon of hope, a kingdom where the people ruled not with greed but with compassion, ensuring that the mistakes of the past would never be repeated.

THE MYSTERY OF GURO FOREST

*I*n the lush green district of Sima, where the air was thick with the scent of wildflowers and the songs of birds, there lay an ancient forest known as Guro. It stood near the gate of Bungueni village, a place of towering trees, tangled vines, and shadows that seemed to stretch forever. To the villagers, Guro was more than just a forest—it was a place of mystery and fear.

Parents warned their children to stay away, telling tales of mischievous jinns who played tricks on those who wandered too close. Hunters spoke of strange noises—growls and roars that sent shivers down their spines. But the most chilling stories were of the children who had vanished over the years. They would wander too close to the forest's edge, lured by the sound of laughter or the sight of glowing lights, only to disappear without a trace.

Among the villagers was a boy named Ankil. He was twelve years old, with a mop of unruly hair and eyes that sparkled with curiosity. While the other children avoided Guro, Ankil was fascinated by it. He spent hours listening to the elders' stories, piecing together fragments of the forest's history.

One evening, as the village gathered around a crackling fire, an elder named Mzee Juma told the tale of Guro. "Long ago," he began, "the forest was a place of peace. But when men began to cut down its trees and hunt its animals, the forest grew angry. It summoned the jinns to protect it, and since then, it has been a place of danger."

Ankil's heart raced as he listened. He couldn't shake the feeling that there was more to the story—something the villagers didn't understand. That night, as he lay in bed, he made a decision. He would uncover the truth about Guro.

The next morning, as the sun rose and painted the sky in hues of gold and pink, Ankil packed a small satchel with bread, a lantern, and his father's old dagger. He slipped out of the village and made his way to the edge of Guro.

The forest was unlike anything he had ever seen. The trees were ancient, their trunks twisted and gnarled, their branches forming a canopy so thick that only faint beams of sunlight broke through. The air was cool and heavy with the scent of earth and moss. Ankil's lantern cast flickering shadows on the ground as he ventured deeper, his heart pounding in his chest.

As he walked, he began to hear whispers—soft, melodious voices that seemed to come from all around him.

"Who dares enter our realm?" a voice hissed, sending a chill down his spine.

Ankil stopped and held up his lantern. "I am Ankil," he said, his voice steady despite his fear. "I seek the truth about Guro."

The air grew colder, and a figure materialized before him. It was a jinn, its form glowing with an ethereal light. Its eyes were silver, shimmering like moonlight on water, and its expression was neither kind nor cruel—simply curious.

"You are brave, young one," the jinn said. "Few dare to enter our domain. What is it you wish to know?"

Ankil hesitated, then asked, "Why do children disappear here? Why does everyone fear this forest?"

The jinn's silver eyes darkened. "The forest is alive, Ankil. It protects itself from harm. Long ago, men sought to destroy Guro for its wood and its treasures. In anger, the forest summoned us, the guardians, to keep intruders away. The children who vanish are not harmed. They are taken to a hidden glade, where they live in peace, far from human greed."

Ankil's eyes widened. "Can I see this glade?"

The jinn studied him for a moment before nodding. With a wave of its hand, the dense trees parted, revealing a hidden world. The glade was bathed in golden light, with sparkling streams, vibrant flowers, and trees that seemed to hum with life. Laughter filled the air as children played, their faces bright and carefree.

Ankil's heart leapt as he spotted familiar faces—children who had been missing from the village for years. Among them was his friend Kito, who had vanished two summers ago.

"Kito!" Ankil called out, running toward him.

Kito turned, his face lighting up with recognition. "Ankil! What are you doing here?"

"I came to find you," Ankil said, his voice trembling with emotion. "Everyone in the village misses you. They think you're gone forever."

Kito's smile faded. "I miss them too. But the jinns said we couldn't go back. They said the forest needed to be protected."

Ankil turned to the jinn. "Can they return home? Their families are heartbroken."

The jinn sighed. "They can, but only if the villagers promise to respect the forest. The balance must be preserved."

Ankil nodded. "I will tell them. I will make them understand."

The jinn placed a hand on Ankil's shoulder. "You are wise beyond your years. Go, and let your people know that the forest is not evil, but it must be respected."

With that, the jinn guided Ankil back to the edge of Guro. The boy returned to the village and gathered everyone in the square. He told them of his journey, the jinns, and the hidden glade. At first, the villagers were skeptical, but when Ankil described the missing children and their joyful lives in the glade, their skepticism turned to hope.

The elders held a meeting and decided to make a pact with the forest. They promised to protect Guro, to plant trees, and to teach their children to respect its mysteries.

The next morning, the villagers gathered at the edge of Guro. Ankil stood at the front, his heart pounding with anticipation. The jinn appeared once more, its silver eyes glowing with approval.

"You have kept your word," it said. "The children may return."

With a wave of its hand, the trees parted, and the missing children emerged, their faces glowing with joy. Families were reunited, tears of happiness streaming down their faces.

From that day on, the villagers of Bungueni lived in harmony with Guro. They planted trees, cared for the land, and taught their children to respect the forest's mysteries. Ankil grew to be a wise leader, known far and wide as the boy who solved the mystery of Guro Forest and brought peace between man and nature.

And so, Guro remained a place of wonder, its secrets known only to those who dared to understand its heart. The laughter of children once again filled the village, and the forest stood as a testament to the power of respect, courage, and the enduring bond between humans and the natural world.

THE CITY OF THE TWO MINARETS

*I*n a city nestled between two great rivers, where the waters shimmered like liquid silver under the sun, stood a magnificent mosque. Its two towering minarets reached toward the heavens, their spires glinting in the light. The mosque was the heart of the city, a place where the faithful gathered to pray, to reflect, and to find solace. But over time, the city had become divided, its people fractured by differences that seemed small but grew into chasms.

The people of the city were all Muslims, but they belonged to two different sects. Each group believed their teachings were the truest path to Allah, and though their differences were minor, they quarreled endlessly. The arguments began in the mosques and spilled into the streets, into the homes, and even into the hearts of the children.

The city became divided, with each group living on opposite sides of the mosque. On Fridays, the two groups would argue over whose call to prayer was more beautiful. During Ramadan, they debated whose fasting traditions were more pure. Even on Eid, a time meant for joy and unity, the city remained split, each group refusing to celebrate with the other.

Children grew up hearing these arguments, and instead of learning love, they learned division. The laughter that once filled the streets was replaced with whispers of suspicion and mistrust. The two minarets, which once symbolized unity under one sky, now seemed to symbolize the division of the people.

In the midst of this strife lived two wise leaders: Imam Rafiq and Sheikh Jamil. Each was the leader of his group, deeply respected by his followers but burdened by the growing divide. Imam Rafiq was a man of quiet strength, his voice calm and his heart full of compassion. Sheikh Jamil was known for his wisdom and his ability to see the bigger picture, even when others could not.

Both men prayed every night for guidance, asking Allah to show them a way to heal their fractured city. One evening, as Imam Rafiq walked through the marketplace, he saw a little girl crying by a broken clay pot. She had dropped it, and the pieces lay scattered on the ground. Moments later, a boy from the other side of the city knelt beside her.

"Don't cry," the boy said softly. "We can fix this together."

The boy and girl, though from different sects, worked side by side, carefully piecing the pot back together. Watching this, Imam Rafiq felt a stirring in his heart. He realized that the children, unburdened by the prejudices of their elders, saw only a shared humanity.

That evening, Imam Rafiq visited Sheikh Jamil. The two men sat in the quiet of the mosque, the moonlight streaming through the stained-glass windows.

"Jamil," Rafiq began, his voice heavy with emotion, "do you see what is happening to our city? We, the leaders, have failed our people. We have taught them division instead of unity."

Sheikh Jamil nodded, his eyes filled with sorrow. "You are right, Rafiq. We have forgotten that it is not our place to judge. Only Allah can decide what is right or wrong. Our duty is to guide our people with love and humility, not pride."

Together, the two leaders came up with a plan. They called for a grand gathering at the mosque, inviting everyone in the city. The people were curious and skeptical, but they came, filling the mosque and spilling out into the courtyard.

Imam Rafiq and Sheikh Jamil stood together before the crowd, a sight no one had ever seen.

"Brothers and sisters," Imam Rafiq began, his voice resonating through the hall, "for too long, we have let our differences divide us. But these differences are minor. We all pray to the same Allah, follow the same Quran, and seek the same path to Paradise."

Sheikh Jamil continued, "It is not for us to judge one another. Only Allah knows what is in our hearts. Our duty as Muslims is to love one another, to show kindness and understanding, and to teach our children that unity is stronger than division."

The people listened in silence, their hearts heavy with the weight of their own actions. Slowly, tears began to flow, and murmurs of agreement rippled through the crowd.

To seal their message, the two leaders led the congregation in a unified prayer, with the voices of both sects rising together in harmony. For the first time in decades, the mosque felt whole, its two minarets no longer symbols of division, but of unity under one sky.

From that day forward, the city began to change. The people celebrated together, prayed together, and taught their children that love and unity were the greatest teachings of all. The little girl and boy from the marketplace grew up to become leaders in their own right, continuing the legacy of peace.

The city flourished, its streets once again filled with laughter and the sounds of children playing. The two minarets stood tall, a reminder that faith is not about division, but about love, understanding, and the shared journey toward Allah.

And so, the City of the Two Minarets became a beacon of hope, a testament to the power of unity and the enduring strength of faith.

THE KINDNESS OF SIMA: A TALE OF BA-IBRAHIM

*I*n the heart of the Comoros, nestled among rolling hills and lush greenery, lies the district of Sima—a place known not only for its breathtaking landscapes but also for the warmth and generosity of its people. It was here, in this tranquil corner of the world, that a man named Ba-Ibrahim found a new home, a new family, and a new purpose.

Ba-Ibrahim was a traveler from the West, a man who had journeyed far and wide in search of something he could not quite name. He had heard whispers of Sima, a place where the air was sweet with the scent of blooming flowers and the people were said to be as kind as they were humble. Curiosity led him to this distant land, though he arrived as a stranger, knowing no one and nothing of the customs or language.

One sunny afternoon, Ba-Ibrahim arrived in Sima Chilindroni, a village within the district. Tired and weary from his journey, he sat beneath the shade of a mango tree, unsure of where to go or what to do. It was there that he met a local man named Mze Ali, a farmer with a weathered face and a smile that radiated warmth.

Mze Ali approached Ba-Ibrahim and, sensing his exhaustion, offered him a drink of fresh coconut water. Though they spoke different languages, the kindness in Mze Ali's eyes transcended words. Through gestures and broken phrases, Ba-Ibrahim shared his story — a tale of wandering, of searching for a place to belong.

Word of the stranger's arrival spread quickly through the village. Soon, a small crowd gathered around Ba-Ibrahim, each person eager to welcome him. Some offered food, others offered shelter, and still others simply smiled, their eyes filled with genuine hospitality.

"Come to my home," said one woman, holding out a basket of ripe fruit. "No, come to mine," insisted another, pointing to a nearby house with a thatched roof. "You must rest at my place," said a young man, his voice filled with enthusiasm.

Ba-Ibrahim was overwhelmed by the kindness of the people. In all his travels, he had never encountered such generosity. Though he was touched by every offer, he felt a deep connection to Mze Ali, the first person who had shown him kindness.

"I will go with him," Ba-Ibrahim said, pointing to Mze Ali. The crowd nodded in understanding, their smiles never fading.

Mze Ali's home was simple but welcoming. His family greeted Ba-Ibrahim with open arms, treating him not as a stranger but as a long-lost relative. They shared meals, stories, and laughter, and though Ba-Ibrahim could not understand every word, he felt the love and warmth in every gesture.

As the days turned into weeks, Ba-Ibrahim grew to love Sima. He marveled at the beauty of the land—the vibrant green fields, the sparkling rivers, and the majestic Mount bounngueni standing tall in the distance. But more than anything, he fell in love with the people. Their kindness, their generosity, and their unwavering sense of community touched his heart in ways he had never imagined.

In time, Ba-Ibrahim decided to make Sima his home. He learned the language, embraced the customs, and became a beloved member of the community. He often reflected on his journey, marveling at how a chance encounter beneath a mango tree had led him to a place where he truly belonged.

Years later, Ba-Ibrahim would tell his story to anyone who would listen. "Sima is more than a place," he would say. "It is a feeling, a warmth that stays with you long after you leave. The people here taught me that kindness is the greatest treasure of all."

And so, Ba-Ibrahim's tale became a legend in Sima, a reminder of the power of hospitality and the beauty of finding home in the most unexpected places. To this day, the people of Sima continue to welcome strangers with open arms, knowing that every act of kindness has the power to change a life.

A LOVE DESTINED BY FATE

*O*nce upon a time, in a bustling village nestled between rolling hills and fertile valleys, there lived a humble and kind-hearted young man named Omar. Though he was poor, his character shone brighter than gold. He was known for his generosity, his gentle nature, and his unwavering faith in Allah. Despite his hardships, Omar never complained, for he believed that his circumstances were a test from the Almighty, and he trusted that one day, his patience and humility would be rewarded.

One sunny afternoon, as Omar was tending to his small garden, a beautiful young woman named Hafswa passed by. She was the daughter of a wealthy merchant, known for her grace, intelligence, and kind heart. As she walked past Omar, their eyes met, and in that moment, something extraordinary happened. Hafswa felt her heart stir in a way it never had before. She was captivated by Omar's gentle demeanor and the sincerity in his eyes. Over the following days, she found herself drawn to him, and soon, she realized she had fallen deeply in love.

One evening, Hafswa gathered her courage and approached Omar. With a trembling voice, she confessed her feelings for him. Omar, though surprised, felt his own heart respond to her words. He, too, had been struck by her beauty and kindness. However, he hesitated, knowing the vast difference in their social standings. "Hafswa," he said gently, "you are the daughter of a wealthy family, and I am but a poor man. Your parents would never approve of us."

But Hafswa was resolute. "Love is not about wealth or status," she replied. "It is about the connection between two hearts. I love you, Omar, and I believe that together, we can overcome any obstacle."

Encouraged by her words, Omar agreed to let their love blossom. For weeks, they met in secret, sharing their dreams and hopes for the future. However, Hafswa knew she could not keep her feelings hidden forever. One day, she decided to tell her parents about Omar. She approached them with a hopeful heart, believing that they would see the goodness in him that she did.

But when Hafswa revealed her love for Omar, her parents were horrified. "How can you marry a poor man?" her mother exclaimed. "You deserve someone who can provide for you, someone of our standing. This Omar is beneath you!"

Her father echoed her mother's sentiments. "If you marry him, we will disown you," he declared. "You will no longer be our daughter."

Hafswa was heartbroken. She loved her parents dearly, but she could not deny her feelings for Omar. Torn between her family and her heart, she went to Omar and tearfully explained the situation. The two lovers wept together, their hearts heavy with sorrow. Omar, though devastated, remained steadfast in his faith. That night, he prayed to Allah, pouring out his heart. "Oh Allah, you are my only hope in this world. You are my only way. I love Hafswa, and I pray that you make her my wife. If it is Your will, please soften the hearts of her parents and unite us in marriage."

Days turned into weeks, and Hafswa's parents remained unmoved. They forbade her from seeing Omar, hoping that time would erase her feelings. But Hafswa's love for Omar only grew stronger. She could not eat, she could not sleep, and her mind was consumed with thoughts of him. Her parents watched in dismay as their once-vibrant daughter grew pale and withdrawn.

One day, Hafswa's resolve broke. She went to her parents and pleaded with them once more. "My mind cannot forget Omar," she cried. "My heart belongs to him, and I cannot imagine a life without him." But her parents remained firm, refusing to give their blessing.

The strain of the situation took its toll on Hafswa. She began to lose her grip on reality, wandering the village and muttering about her love for Omar. Her parents were devastated, realizing too late the consequences of their actions. They had driven their daughter to madness in their stubbornness.

Meanwhile, Omar, heartbroken but still deeply in love with Hafswa, continued to pray for her well-being. One day, as he was walking through the village, he saw Hafswa in her distressed state. His heart ached for her, and he knew he could not abandon her. He went to her parents once more, this time with a humble yet determined request.

"I love Hafswa," he said. "I know she is unwell, but my love for her has not wavered. I ask for your permission to marry her and care for her for the rest of my days."

Hafswa's parents were overcome with guilt and shame. They realized that their pride and prejudice had caused their daughter's suffering. With tears in their eyes, they asked Omar, "Will you truly marry someone who has lost her mind? We feel deeply guilty for what has happened to our daughter."

Omar smiled gently. "Love has no boundaries," he replied. "I will care for Hafswa and cherish her, no matter what."

Touched by his sincerity, Hafswa's parents finally gave their blessing. The wedding was arranged, and on the day of the ceremony, something miraculous happened.

As Omar placed the wedding ring on Hafswa's finger, a spark of clarity returned to her eyes. She looked at Omar and smiled her mind and heart restored. The villagers rejoiced, and Hafswa's parents wept tears of joy, grateful for the second chance they had been given.

Omar and Hafswa began their life together, filled with love and gratitude. Omar continued to work hard, and with Hafswa's support, their fortunes began to improve. They were happy, but little did they know that their lives were about to change in ways they could never have imagined.

One day, as Omar was walking to the mosque for his prayers, he encountered an old man sitting by the roadside. The man's eyes widened in recognition as he looked at Omar. "You... you are the spitting image of King Hakim," the old man whispered.

Omar was puzzled. "King Hakim? I am but a humble man, sir. I do not know of any king."

✦ ✦ ✦

The old man's eyes filled with tears. "Many years ago, I was a servant in the palace of King Hakim. His wife, the queen, gave birth to a son, but she feared for the child's life due to a prophecy. She ordered me to take the baby away and hide him. I did as I was told, but I have lived with the guilt of my actions ever since. You, Omar, are that child. You are the lost prince of the kingdom."

Omar was stunned. He could not believe what he was hearing. The old man insisted on taking him to the palace, where he recounted the story to King Hakim. The king, overcome with emotion, embraced Omar as his long-lost son. The kingdom rejoiced at the return of their prince, and Omar's life was transformed overnight.

Despite his newfound status, Omar remained humble and kind. He brought Hafswa to the palace, where she was welcomed as a princess. Together, they ruled with wisdom and compassion, ensuring that their people were cared for and that justice prevailed.

Omar never forgot his roots or the lessons he had learned during his years of hardship. He often reflected on the trials he and Hafswa had endured, grateful for the love and faith that had carried them through. And so, the humble poor man and the merchant's daughter became the beloved king and queen of the land, their love story inspiring generations to come. And they lived happily ever after.

A LOVE THAT CROSSED BORDERS

Once upon a time, in a small, close-knit village surrounded by lush green fields and towering mountains, there lived a young man named Ahmed. Ahmed was known for his intelligence, ambition, and kind heart. He had always dreamed of pursuing higher education abroad, hoping to one day return to his village and contribute to its growth and development. His parents, though proud of his aspirations, were traditional in their ways and believed in the customs of their ancestors. Before Ahmed left for his studies, they arranged a marriage for him with a young woman from their village, a practice common in their culture.

Ahmed, however, was not ready for marriage. He had never met his fiancée, and though she was said to be kind and beautiful, he felt no connection to her. He tried to explain his feelings to his parents, but they insisted that the arrangement was for the best. Reluctantly, Ahmed agreed to the engagement, but deep down, he knew his heart was not in it. With a heavy heart, he bid farewell to his family and set off for a distant land to pursue his dreams.

In the bustling city where Ahmed began his studies, he found himself immersed in a world of new experiences and opportunities. He worked hard, excelling in his studies, but he often felt lonely and homesick. One day, while walking through a park near his university, he noticed a young woman sitting on a bench, reading a book. She had a radiant smile and an air of confidence that immediately caught his attention. Her name was Anabela.

✛ ✛ ✛

Anabela was kind, intelligent, and full of life. She and Ahmed quickly became friends, spending hours talking about their dreams, their cultures, and their lives. Over time, their friendship blossomed into love. Ahmed found himself falling deeply for Anabela, and she felt the same way about him. However, Ahmed was torn. He knew he had a fiancée back home, and though he had never loved her, he felt a sense of duty to his family and their traditions.

One evening, as Ahmed and Anabela sat by the river, watching the sunset, Ahmed confessed his dilemma. "Anabela," he said, his voice trembling, "I love you more than anything, but I have a fiancée back home. I don't know what to do. I don't want to hurt my family, but I can't imagine a life without you."

Anabela listened patiently, her heart aching for Ahmed. "Love is not something we can control," she said gently. "But we must be true to ourselves and to those we care about. Whatever you decide, I will support you."

Ahmed knew he had to make a choice. After much soul-searching, he decided to follow his heart and be with Anabela. He wrote a letter to his parents, explaining his feelings and asking for their understanding. However, before he could send the letter, he received news from home. His fiancée had married someone else. Ahmed was shocked but also relieved. He realized that his parents' arrangement had never been meant to be, and he felt a sense of freedom he had not known before.

With a lighter heart, Ahmed and Anabela continued their life together. Their love grew stronger with each passing day, and soon, they were blessed with a beautiful baby boy. Ahmed was overjoyed, but he knew it was time to share the news with his parents. He wrote a heartfelt letter to his mother, telling her about Anabela and their son. He explained how happy he was and how much he hoped she would accept his new family.

Weeks passed, and Ahmed anxiously awaited a response. Finally, a letter arrived from his mother. With trembling hands, he opened it and began to read. To his surprise and relief, his mother's words were filled with love and joy.

"My dearest Ahmed," she wrote, "I cannot express how happy I am to hear your news. All these years, I have carried a heavy burden in my heart. Months after you left, your fiancée married another man. I was worried about how you would feel when you found out, and I feared it would hurt you. But now, knowing that you have found love and happiness with Anabela, and that you have a beautiful son, my heart is at peace. I am so proud of you, my son, and I cannot wait to meet my grandson and your beloved Anabela."

Tears filled Ahmed's eyes as he read his mother's words. He felt a wave of relief and gratitude wash over him. He showed the letter to Anabela, and together, they celebrated the love and acceptance that had bridged the distance between them and Ahmed's family.

☩ ☩ ☩

In the months that followed, Ahmed, Anabela, and their son traveled to Ahmed's village to meet his parents. The reunion was filled with joy and laughter. Ahmed's mother embraced Anabela as if she were her own daughter, and she cradled her grandson with tears of happiness in her eyes. The entire village celebrated the return of Ahmed and the arrival of his new family.

Ahmed's story became a tale of love, courage, and the power of following one's heart. He and Anabela built a life filled with love and happiness, honoring both their traditions and their dreams. And as their son grew, they taught him the importance of kindness, understanding, and the belief that love knows no boundaries.

And so, Ahmed, Anabela, and their little family lived happily ever after, their hearts forever connected by the bonds of love and the acceptance of those who mattered most.

BEYOND THE SURFACE

Once upon a time, in a quiet village nestled between rolling hills and a sparkling blue sea, there lived a young man named Kofi. Kofi was known for his charm, his strong will, and his tendency to act on impulse. His parents, wise and kind, often tried to guide him with their words of wisdom, but Kofi, like many young men, believed he knew best.

One evening, as the sun dipped below the horizon, painting the sky in hues of orange and pink, Kofi's parents sat him down for a heartfelt conversation. "My son," his father began, "a good wife is not about beauty alone. It is about her heart, her character, and her values. Take your time to know a woman before you decide to spend your life with her."

His mother nodded in agreement. "Love is not just about what you see with your eyes, Kofi. It is about what you feel in your soul and what you build together over time. Do not rush into marriage without understanding the person you are marrying."

Kofi listened politely, but deep down, he dismissed their advice. He was young, confident, and certain that he knew what he wanted. Little did he know, his life was about to take a turn that would teach him the true meaning of his parents' words.

One sunny afternoon, Kofi decided to take a walk along the beach. The waves crashed gently against the shore, and the salty breeze filled the air. As he strolled, he noticed a woman sitting on a rock, her long hair flowing in the wind, her beauty striking. Her name was Adwoa, and she was the most beautiful woman Kofi had ever seen. At that moment, he felt his heart leap, and he was convinced he had found the love of his life.

Without hesitation, Kofi approached Adwoa and struck up a conversation. She was charming and witty, and Kofi was captivated. Over the next few days, they spent hours together, talking and laughing. Kofi was so enamored by Adwoa's beauty and charm that he never stopped to ask himself if he truly knew her. He never considered her values, her habits, or her character. All he saw was her outward appearance, and that was enough for him.

One evening, Kofi announced to his parents that he had found the woman he wanted to marry. His parents were surprised and concerned. "Kofi," his father said, "have you taken the time to know her? Marriage is a lifelong commitment. It is not something to rush into."

Kofi waved off their concerns. "I love her, and that's all that matters," he replied confidently. "I don't need to know anything else."

His mother tried to reason with him. "Please, Kofi, take your time. Get to know her better. Love is not just about feelings; it is about understanding and respect."

But Kofi was adamant. He was determined to marry Adwoa, and nothing his parents said could change his mind. Reluctantly, his parents gave their blessing, hoping that their son's happiness would prove them wrong.

The wedding was a grand affair, filled with music, dancing, and celebration. Kofi was overjoyed, convinced that he had made the right choice. But as the days turned into weeks, cracks began to appear in his perfect picture of married life.

Adwoa, though beautiful, was not the partner Kofi had imagined. She was lazy and selfish, expecting Kofi to do all the household chores after a long day of work. When Kofi would leave for work in the mornings, Adwoa would invite other men into their home, spending hours chatting and laughing with them instead of tending to her responsibilities. Kofi, blinded by his initial infatuation, tried to ignore these red flags, but deep down, he began to feel a growing sense of unease.

One day, Kofi returned home earlier than usual. As he approached the house, he heard laughter and voices coming from inside. Peering through the window, he saw Adwoa sitting with a group of men, chatting and drinking as if she didn't have a care in the world. Kofi's heart sank as he realized the truth about his wife. She had been using him, taking advantage of his kindness and devotion.

Feeling a mix of anger, shame, and regret, Kofi confronted Adwoa. "How could you do this to me?" he demanded. "I trusted you, and this is how you repay me?"

Adwoa shrugged her expression indifferent. "You married me for my beauty, Kofi. Did you really think that was enough to build a life together?"

Her words struck Kofi like a blow. He realized then that his parents had been right all along. He had been so focused on Adwoa's outward appearance that he had failed to see the truth about her character. He had rushed into marriage without taking the time to truly know her, and now he was paying the price.

✛ ✛ ✛

With a heavy heart, Kofi went to his parents and confessed everything. "I was wrong," he said, his voice filled with shame. "I didn't listen to your advice, and now I see the consequences of my actions. I married Adwoa without knowing who she truly was, and now I am suffering for it."

His parents listened with compassion, their hearts aching for their son. "Kofi," his father said gently, "we all make mistakes. What matters is what you learn from them. Use this experience to grow and to understand the importance of patience and wisdom."

Kofi nodded, tears in his eyes. "I will," he promised. "I will never again judge someone based on appearances alone. I will take the time to know a person's heart before making such an important decision."

In the months that followed, Kofi worked to rebuild his life. He and Adwoa parted ways, and though the experience was painful, it taught him valuable lessons about love, trust, and the importance of listening to those who care for him.

Years later, Kofi met a woman named Efia. She was not as strikingly beautiful as Adwoa, but her kindness, intelligence, and warmth captured Kofi's heart. This time, he took his time to get to know her, to understand her values and her character. When he finally asked her to marry him, it was with the confidence that he had found a true partner, someone who would stand by his side through thick and thin.

Kofi's parents smiled with pride as they watched their son grow into a wiser, more thoughtful man. And as Kofi and Efia began their life together, they built a marriage rooted in love, respect, and understanding—a marriage that would stand the test of time.

And so, Kofi's story became a lesson for the entire village: that true love is not about beauty alone, but about the beauty of the heart. And those who take the time to seek it will find a love that lasts a lifetime.

THE CURSE OF BEAUTY

O nce upon a time, in a bustling kingdom surrounded by lush forests and sparkling rivers, there lived two cousins who were as different as night and day. Amina was kind-hearted, gentle, and full of compassion. Her beauty was not just in her appearance but in her soul, which radiated warmth and love to everyone she met. Her cousin, Mamana, on the other hand, was cunning, jealous, and consumed by bitterness. Though she was beautiful on the outside, her heart was dark, and she would stop at nothing to get what she wanted.

The kingdom they lived in had a unique tradition: every year, the royal family would choose the most beautiful men and women to marry into their lineage. It was considered a great honor, and many young people dreamed of being chosen. Mamana, driven by her ambition and envy, was determined to secure a place in the royal family for herself and her children. Amina, however, had no such desires. She was content with her simple life, helping others and spreading kindness wherever she went.

One day, as fate would have it, Amina met a young man named Yusuf. He was the most handsome man anyone had ever seen, with a smile that could light up the darkest night. But more than his looks, Yusuf was kind, humble, and hardworking. Amina and Yusuf quickly became close friends, and over time, their friendship blossomed into love. Mamana, however, could not stand to see her cousin happy. Consumed by jealousy, she devised a wicked plan.

Mamana sought out a powerful witch who lived deep in the forest. "I want you to curse Yusuf," Mamana demanded. "I want him to suffer, but I also want his beauty to grow so that he becomes the most handsome man in the kingdom. I want him to be so beautiful that no one can resist him, but I want him to be cursed with misfortune."

The witch, intrigued by Mamana's malice, agreed. She cast a spell on Yusuf, causing him to grow thinner and weaker with each passing day. But as his health declined, his beauty intensified. His eyes became more radiant, his features more striking, and his presence more captivating. People in the kingdom began to whisper about the cursed man who was both the most beautiful and the most unfortunate.

Amina was heartbroken to see Yusuf suffer. She tried everything to break the curse, but nothing worked. Mamana, meanwhile, reveled in her cousin's pain. She had her own children, whom she hoped would one day marry into the royal family. But despite her efforts, her children were not blessed with beauty or charm. They were ordinary, and Mamana's dreams of grandeur seemed further out of reach.

Meanwhile, in the royal palace, the king's daughter, Princess Mariam, began to have strange dreams. Night after night, she dreamt of a man so handsome that his beauty seemed otherworldly. In her dreams, he was kind and gentle, and she felt an inexplicable connection to him. When she told her father, King Fazul, about the dreams, he dismissed them. "It is just a dream, my dear," he said. "How can you dream of someone you have never seen?"

But the dreams persisted. Night after night, Princess Mariam saw the same man, and she became convinced that he was real. Finally, she went to her father again. "Father, I cannot ignore these dreams. I believe this man exists, and I must find him."

King Fazul, though skeptical, loved his daughter dearly and wanted to make her happy. He issued a decree: all the young men in the kingdom were to be brought to the palace so that Princess Mariam could see if her dream man was among them.

The day of the gathering arrived, and the palace courtyard was filled with young men from every corner of the kingdom. They stood in rows, each hoping to catch the princess's eye. Princess Mariam walked among them, her heart pounding with anticipation. But as she looked into each face, she felt nothing. None of them were the man from her dreams.

King Fazul, growing impatient, asked his daughter, "Have you found him? Is he here?"

+ + +

Princess Mariam shook her head, tears welling in her eyes. "No, Father. He is not here."

The king, determined to fulfill his daughter's wish, ordered his guards to search every village, every home, and every corner of the kingdom. "Bring every young man to the palace," he commanded. "No one is to be left out."

The guards scoured the land, and finally, they came to Yusuf's village. When they saw him, they were struck by his beauty, even in his weakened state. They brought him to the palace, and as soon as Princess Mariam saw him, her heart leapt with joy. "Father," she whispered, "this is him. This is the man from my dreams."

King Fazul was astonished. He had never seen anyone so beautiful, yet so frail. He approached Yusuf and asked, "Who are you, young man? And why do you look so ill?"

Yusuf, too weak to stand, bowed his head and said, "Your Majesty, I am Yusuf. I have been cursed by a witch, and though my beauty grows, my strength fades."

Princess Mariam, moved by compassion, knelt beside Yusuf. "Father," she said, "we must help him. I believe he is the one I am meant to be with."

King Fazul, though hesitant, could not deny the connection between his daughter and Yusuf. He called for the kingdom's wisest healers and sorcerers to break the curse. After many attempts, they discovered that the curse could only be lifted by an act of true love.

Amina, who had followed Yusuf to the palace, stepped forward. "I love Yusuf," she said. "I have loved him since the day we met. If my love can break the curse, then let it be so."

As Amina spoke, a bright light enveloped Yusuf. His strength returned, and the curse was lifted. Princess Mariam, though heartbroken, realized that Yusuf's heart belonged to Amina. She stepped aside, knowing that true love could not be forced.

Yusuf and Amina were married in a grand ceremony, and their love became a legend in the kingdom. Mamana, exposed for her wickedness, was banished from the kingdom, her dreams of power and glory shattered.

As for Princess Mariam, she eventually found her own true love, a kind and noble man who had been by her side all along. The kingdom prospered, and the tale of the cursed man who became the luckiest in the city was told for generations, a reminder that true beauty lies in the heart, and that love, kindness, and compassion will always triumph over envy and malice.

And so, Yusuf and Amina lived happily ever after, their love a beacon of hope and inspiration for all who heard their story.

BENEATH DIVIDED SKIES

*O*nce upon a time, in a vast and fertile land, there was a country known for its generosity and kindness. The people of this land, called the Amara, were known far and wide for their open hearts and willingness to help those in need. They believed in unity, compassion, and the idea that all people, regardless of their differences, deserved respect and dignity.

One day, a group of travelers arrived at the borders of Amara. They were from a distant land, fleeing persecution and hardship in their own country. Their skin was a different shade, their language unfamiliar, and their customs strange to the Amara people. But the Amara, true to their nature, welcomed the travelers with open arms. They provided them with food, shelter, and land to cultivate, treating them as equals despite their differences in culture and religion.

For many years, the two groups lived side by side, the Amara sharing their resources and knowledge with the newcomers, whom they called the Zorai. The Zorai, grateful at first, began to build their lives in this new land. However, as time passed, some among the Zorai began to grow restless. Instead of showing gratitude for the kindness they had received, they started to resent the Amara, viewing them as naive and weak. They began to take more than their share, encroaching on Amara lands and resources. Over time, they seized a third of the Amara's territory, claiming it as their own.

The Amara, heartbroken and betrayed, tried to reason with the Zorai, reminding them of the hospitality they had been shown. But the Zorai, now emboldened, refused to listen. They mocked the Amara, calling them foolish for trusting outsiders. The once-harmonious relationship between the two groups deteriorated into mistrust and hostility.

Amidst this turmoil, there lived a young Amara man named Abbas. Abbas was kind-hearted and optimistic, always seeing the good in people. One day, while walking through the market, he saw a young Zorai woman named Janet. She was strikingly beautiful, with a gentle smile and eyes that seemed to hold the wisdom of the stars. Abbas was immediately captivated. Over time, he found himself falling deeply in love with her.

Janet, too, was drawn to Abbas. She was different from many of her people—kind, humble, and deeply empathetic. She had always felt out of place among the

Zorai, who had become increasingly aggressive and ungrateful. She admired the Amara for their generosity and wished for peace between the two groups.

One evening, Abbas decided to tell his parents about his feelings for Janet. He sat them down and said, "Mother, Father, I have met someone who has captured my heart. Her name is Janet, and she is a Zorai. I know there is tension between our people, but she is different. She is kind and good, and I believe she could be the one for me."

His parents exchanged worried glances. His father, a wise and respected elder, spoke first. "Abbas, my son, I understand your feelings, but you must think carefully. The Zorai have taken so much from us. They have shown no gratitude for our kindness. How can you marry someone from a people who have treated us so poorly?"

✛ ✛ ✛

His mother added, "It is not just about Janet, Abbas. It is about the actions of her people. They have stolen our lands, disrespected our traditions, and betrayed our trust. How can we welcome one of them into our family?"

Abbas felt a pang of sadness but remained steadfast. "Janet is not like the others," he insisted. "She is innocent. She does not agree with what her people have done. Should she be punished for their actions? Love knows no boundaries, and I believe she could help bridge the gap between our people."

His parents were silent for a long time, their faces etched with concern. Finally, his father sighed and said, "Abbas, we trust your judgment, but we fear for you. The wounds between our people run deep. If you choose to pursue this path, you must be prepared for the challenges that will come."

Abbas nodded, grateful for their understanding. He knew it would not be easy, but he was determined to follow his heart. He continued to see Janet in secret, their love growing stronger with each passing day. Janet, too, faced criticism from her own people, who accused her of betraying them by associating with an Amara. But she, like Abbas, believed that love could overcome hatred.

One day, as tensions between the Amara and the Zorai reached a boiling point, Abbas and Janet decided to take a bold step. They stood before both communities, hand in hand, and declared their love for each other. "We are proof that our people can coexist," Abbas said. "We may have different customs and histories, but we share the same heart. Let us not allow the mistakes of the past to dictate our future."

Janet added, "I may be Zorai, but I stand with the Amara in their call for peace and justice. My people have wronged them, and for that, I am deeply sorry. But let us not repeat those mistakes. Let us build a future where we can live together in harmony."

Their words stirred something in the hearts of both the Amara and the Zorai. Slowly, people began to see the possibility of reconciliation. The elders of both communities came together to discuss a way forward, guided by the love and courage of Abbas and Janet.

Over time, the two groups began to heal. The Zorai returned the lands they had taken and worked to rebuild the trust they had broken. The Amara, true to their nature, forgave them, choosing to focus on the future rather than the past. Abbas and Janet's love became a symbol of hope and unity, inspiring others to look beyond their differences and embrace what they had in common.

Years later, Abbas and Janet stood together, watching their children play with both Amara and Zorai friends. The land that had once been divided was now united, a testament to the power of love, forgiveness, and the belief that even the deepest wounds can heal.

And so, the tale of Abbas and Janet became a legend, reminding all who heard it that love knows no boundaries and that even in the face of hatred and division, there is always hope for a brighter tomorrow.

FROM OUTCAST
TO TRIUMPH

*O*nce upon a time, in a small, remote village nestled between rolling hills and dense forests, there lived a man named Maolana. Maolana was a hardworking and kind-hearted man, but he was often overlooked by the people of his village. Despite his best efforts, he struggled to find a wife. Every time he expressed interest in a woman, he was met with rejection. The villagers would whisper behind his back, saying he was unlucky or cursed. Maolana, though disheartened, never let their words break his spirit. He continued to work hard, tending to his farm and helping others whenever he could.

One day, after yet another rejection, Maolana decided he could no longer stay in the village that had brought him so much pain. He packed his few belongings and set off for a nearby village, hoping to start anew. As he walked through the forest, he felt a mix of sadness and hope. He wondered if he would ever find a place where he belonged.

When Maolana arrived at the neighboring village, he was struck by its beauty. The people seemed friendly, and the air was filled with the scent of blooming flowers. As he wandered through the village, he noticed a young woman drawing water from a well. She was the most beautiful woman he had ever seen, with a radiant smile and eyes that sparkled like the stars. Her name was Maimuna.

Maolana gathered his courage and approached her. "Good day," he said, his voice trembling slightly. "My name is Maolana. I am new to this village, and I was wondering if you would allow me to take you on a date."

Maimuna looked at him, surprised but intrigued. She had never been approached so boldly, but there was something about Maolana's sincerity that touched her heart. After a moment's hesitation, she smiled and said, "I would be honored, Maolana."

Their first date was magical. They talked for hours, sharing their dreams and stories. Maolana told Maimuna about his struggles in his old village, and she listened with empathy and kindness. Maimuna, in turn, shared her own dreams of a life filled with love and adventure. By the end of the evening, both of them knew they had found something special.

Over the following months, Maolana and Maimuna grew closer. Their love blossomed, and soon, they decided to marry. The wedding was a joyous occasion, celebrated by the entire village. Maolana, who had once felt like an outcast, now felt like he had found his true home.

After their marriage, Maolana and Maimuna worked together to build a life filled with love and prosperity. Maolana started a small business, trading goods between villages. His hard work and determination paid off, and his business grew rapidly. Before long, he became the wealthiest man in the village. He and Maimuna were blessed with several children, and their family became a symbol of happiness and success.

Years passed, and Maolana's life was filled with joy and fulfillment. But deep down, he never forgot his roots. He often thought about his parents and the village where he had grown up. One day, he decided it was time to return and see his family. He packed a cart with treasures— gold, silks, and other precious gifts—and set off for his old village with Maimuna and their children by his side.

When Maolana arrived in his old village, the people were astonished. The man they had once rejected and ridiculed was now a wealthy and successful merchant, accompanied by a beautiful wife and children. The villagers gathered around, their eyes wide with admiration and envy.

Maolana went straight to his parents' home. When they saw him, they wept with joy. They had missed their son dearly and were overjoyed to see him return with such blessings. Maolana presented them with the treasures he had brought, and they embraced him, grateful for his love and generosity.

As word spread through the village, people began to approach Maolana, offering their congratulations and apologies. "We were wrong to treat you the way we did," they said. "You have proven that true success comes from hard work and perseverance."

Maolana, ever humble, accepted their apologies with grace. "The past is behind us," he said. "What matters now is that we move forward together."

Despite the warm welcome, Maolana knew that his true home was now with Maimuna and their children in the neighboring village. He spent a few days with his parents, catching up on lost time, before bidding them farewell. "I will visit often," he promised, "but my life is with my family now."

As Maolana and his family prepared to leave, the villagers gathered to see them off. They waved and cheered, their hearts filled with admiration for the man who had once been an outcast but had returned as a hero.

Maolana's journey became a legend in both villages. His story was told and retold, a reminder that true success is not measured by wealth or status, but by love, kindness, and the courage to follow one's dreams. And so, Maolana and Maimuna lived happily ever after, their love and perseverance inspiring generations to come.

ETERNAL LOVE

*O*nce upon a time, in a serene village nestled beside a winding river, there lived a man named Nakiddi. He was known for his gentle heart, his unwavering kindness, and his deep love for his wife, Amina. Amina was the light of Nakiddi's life — a woman of unparalleled beauty, both in appearance and in spirit. Her laughter was like music, and her presence brought warmth to everyone around her. The two of them were inseparable, their love a beacon of hope and joy in the village.

Nakiddi and Amina lived a simple yet fulfilling life. They spent their days tending to their small farm, sharing stories by the fire, and dreaming of a future filled with children and laughter. Their love was the kind that poets wrote about, a love that transcended time and space. But fate, as it often does, had other plans.

+ + +

One fateful day, Amina fell gravely ill. Her condition worsened rapidly, and it became clear that she needed urgent medical attention. The nearest hospital was across the river, and the only way to reach it was by boat. Nakiddi, desperate to save his beloved, carried Amina to the riverbank, where a small boat awaited them. The river was known for its treacherous currents, but Nakiddi was willing to risk anything for Amina.

As they set out across the river, the sky darkened, and a fierce storm began to brew. The wind howled, and the waves grew higher and more violent. Despite Nakiddi's best efforts to steady the boat, a massive wave crashed over them, capsizing the vessel. Nakiddi fought to keep Amina afloat, but the current was too strong. In a moment of heart-wrenching despair, Amina slipped from his grasp and disappeared beneath the raging waters.

Nakiddi was pulled to safety by villagers who had witnessed the tragedy from the shore, but Amina was gone. Her body was never found, and Nakiddi was left with nothing but the memory of her smile and the sound of her laughter. The villagers tried to console him, but Nakiddi's grief was too deep. He felt as though the world had betrayed him, taking away the one person who had made his life worth living.

For days, Nakiddi refused to eat or sleep. He sat by the river, staring at the water as if hoping Amina would emerge from its depths. He cried until he had no tears left, his heart shattered into a thousand pieces. "Why?"

he whispered to the heavens. "Why did you take her from me? She was my everything."

In his anguish, Nakiddi made a vow. He would never marry again. Amina would remain in his heart forever, her memory a sacred treasure that no one could replace. He began to live as though she were still by his side, setting a place for her at the table and speaking to her as if she could hear him. To Nakiddi, Amina's body may have perished, but her soul was eternal, a constant presence in his life.

As the years passed, Nakiddi's devotion to Amina's memory became legendary in the village. Many women, touched by his loyalty and moved by his story, approached him, hoping to win his heart. But Nakiddi remained steadfast in his vow. "Amina is my wife," he would say. "She may no longer be here in body, but her soul is with me always. I cannot betray her memory."

Nakiddi's nights were filled with dreams of Amina. In his dreams, she was as radiant as ever, her laughter echoing in his ears. She would take his hand and lead him through fields of golden flowers, their love as vibrant as it had been in life. These dreams were both a blessing and a curse, for they brought him comfort but also deepened his longing for her.

One night, as Nakiddi slept, he had a particularly vivid dream. Amina appeared before him, her eyes filled with love and sorrow. "My dearest Nakiddi," she said, her voice soft and melodic, "you have carried me in your heart for so long. But now it is time for you to let go. I will always love you, but you must live your life. Find happiness, not for my sake, but for yours."

Nakiddi woke with a start, his heart pounding. He sat by the window, staring at the moon as tears streamed down his face. Amina's words echoed in his mind, and for the first time in years, he felt a glimmer of hope. Perhaps she was right. Perhaps it was time to honor her memory by living a life filled with love and joy, just as she would have wanted.

The next morning, Nakiddi went to the riverbank, where he had spent so many hours mourning Amina. He knelt by the water and whispered, "I will always love you, Amina. But I will also honor your wish. I will live my life, not in sorrow, but in gratitude for the love we shared."

From that day forward, Nakiddi began to heal. He opened his heart to the world, finding joy in the simple pleasures of life. He continued to cherish Amina's memory, but he also allowed himself to embrace the possibility of new love. The villagers, who had long admired his devotion, celebrated his transformation.

Years later, Nakiddi met a kind and gentle woman named Zainab. She had heard his story and was moved by his strength and resilience. Slowly, Nakiddi and Zainab built a life together, their love rooted in mutual respect and understanding. Nakiddi never forgot Amina, but he learned that love is not finite — it grows and expands, embracing new possibilities while honoring the past.

Nakiddi's story became a legend in the village, a tale of love, loss, and the enduring power of the human spirit. And though Amina was no longer by his side, her presence remained in his heart, a guiding light that led him to a life of love, hope, and fulfillment.

BEYOND SIGHT

*O*nce upon a time, in a remote and majestic mountain range, there lived a young man named Halid. Halid was born blind, but his lack of sight did not diminish his inner and outer beauty. He had a striking presence, with sharp features, a warm smile, and a heart full of kindness. Despite his blindness, Halid had learned to navigate the mountains with remarkable skill, using his other senses to connect with the world around him. He lived a simple life, content with the rhythms of nature and the peacefulness of his surroundings.

One day, a young woman named Mwana Aisha, the daughter of a wealthy merchant from the nearby town, decided to take a walk in the mountains. She had always been drawn to the beauty of the peaks, the crisp air, and the sense of freedom they offered. As she wandered along a narrow path, she came across Halid, who was sitting on a rock, listening to the sounds of the wind and the birds. Mwana Aisha was immediately struck by his beauty. His face seemed to glow with an inner light, and his presence was both calming and captivating.

Mwana Aisha stood there for a moment, unsure of what to do. She had never felt such a strong connection to anyone before. Finally, she gathered her courage and approached him. "Hello," she said softly. "My name is Mwana Aisha. May I sit with you?"

Halid turned his head toward her voice and smiled. "Of course," he replied. "I am Halid. It's a pleasure to meet you."

The two of them began to talk, and Mwana Aisha was amazed by Halid's wisdom, his gentle nature, and his ability to see the world in ways she had never imagined. Though he could not see with his eyes, he described the mountains, the sky, and the flowers with such vividness that Mwana Aisha felt as though she were seeing them for the first time. By the time they parted ways, Mwana Aisha knew she had found the love of her life.

When Mwana Aisha returned home, she went straight to her father, a stern and powerful man named Ibrahim. "Father," she said, her voice trembling with excitement, "I think I have found the love of my life."

Ibrahim raised an eyebrow. "Oh? And who is this man? Did you speak to him about your feelings?"

"Not yet," Mwana Aisha admitted. "But I will. He is unlike anyone I have ever met."

The next day, Mwana Aisha returned to the mountains and found Halid in the same spot. She sat beside him and took a deep breath. "Halid," she began, "I must tell you something. I have fallen in love with you."

Halid was silent for a moment, his expression unreadable. Finally, he spoke. "Mwana Aisha, you are kind and beautiful, but how can you love a blind man? I cannot give you the life you deserve. I cannot see the world as you do."

Mwana Aisha reached out and took his hand. "Love is not about what the eyes can see," she said firmly. "It is about what the heart feels. I love you, Halid, not for your sight, but for your soul."

Halid's heart swelled with emotion. He had never imagined that someone could love him so deeply, so unconditionally. "If you truly feel this way," he said, "then I accept your love. But we must face the challenges ahead together."

Mwana Aisha nodded. "We will. But first, we must tell my father."

When Mwana Aisha brought Halid to meet her father, Ibrahim was furious. "How can you bring a blind man into my home?" he shouted. "Do you think I will allow my daughter to marry someone like him?"

Mwana Aisha stood her ground. "Father, I love Halid. He is the man I choose to spend my life with. If you cannot accept him, then I will leave with him."

Ibrahim's face turned red with anger. "If that is your choice, then go. But know that you will no longer be my daughter."

Mwana Aisha's heart ached, but she knew she could not abandon Halid. She took his hand and left her father's house, determined to build a life with the man she loved.

The two of them returned to the mountains, where they were married in a simple ceremony surrounded by nature. As they exchanged vows, a miracle occurred. Halid's vision was restored, and for the first time, he saw the world in all its beauty. He looked at Mwana Aisha, his eyes filled with tears of joy. "You are even more beautiful than I imagined," he whispered.

Mwana Aisha laughed, her heart overflowing with happiness. "And now you can see the world as I do."

✛ ✛ ✛

Over the years, Halid and Mwana Aisha built a life together filled with love, laughter, and prosperity. Halid's newfound vision allowed him to expand his skills, and he became a successful craftsman, creating beautiful works of art that were sought after far and wide. They were blessed with many children, and their home in the mountains became a place of warmth and joy.

One day, Ibrahim heard rumors of Halid's miraculous healing and the success he and Mwana Aisha had found. Shame filled his heart as he realized how wrong he had been to judge Halid. Swallowing his pride, he traveled to the mountains to seek forgiveness.

When he arrived at their home, Mwana Aisha was surprised to see him. "Father," she said, her voice tinged with both joy and sorrow. "What brings you here?"

Ibrahim bowed his head. "I have come to ask for your forgiveness," he said. "I was wrong to judge Halid and to turn you away. I see now that love is not about what the eyes can see, but about what the heart knows. Please, forgive me."

Mwana Aisha's eyes filled with tears. She embraced her father, and Halid joined them, his heart full of compassion. "You are forgiven," Halid said. "We are family, and family should always be together."

From that day forward, Ibrahim became a part of their lives, learning to see the world through Halid's eyes and finding joy in the love and happiness his daughter had built. And so, Halid and Mwana Aisha's story became a legend, a tale of love, forgiveness, and the miracles that can happen when we follow our hearts. And they lived happily ever after.

THE HEART'S DECREE

*O*nce upon a time, in a prosperous kingdom surrounded by lush forests and sparkling rivers, there lived a wise and just king named Rachad. He ruled with fairness and compassion, and his people loved him dearly. King Rachad had a son named Ali, a young man known for his intelligence, kindness, and striking appearance. Ali was the pride of the kingdom, and everyone believed he would one day become a great ruler.

However, not everyone in the kingdom had good intentions. In a dark corner of the land, there lived a cunning witch named Zoraya. Zoraya was known for her deceitful ways and her desire for power. She had a daughter named Fanara, who, despite her mother's beauty, was not blessed with charm or grace. Zoraya was determined to see her daughter marry into the royal family, believing it would elevate her own status and secure her influence over the kingdom.

One day, Zoraya devised a wicked plan. She traveled to the palace and requested an audience with King Rachad. When she was brought before him, she bowed low and said, "Your Majesty, I bring grave news. I have had a vision, and it foretells the downfall of your kingdom."

King Rachad, alarmed, leaned forward. "What do you mean? What have you seen?"

Zoraya's eyes gleamed with mischief as she spun her tale. "I saw your son, Prince Ali, marrying a woman who will bring ruin to this land. Her presence will sow discord and lead to the collapse of your reign."

The king's face paled. "What can I do to prevent this?" he asked.

Zoraya pretended to think deeply. "Bring me two eggs," she said. "With them, I can perform a ritual to uncover the truth and guide you on the path to salvation."

The king, desperate to protect his kingdom, agreed. The next day, he brought two eggs to Zoraya, unaware that she had already prepared a deceitful scheme. Zoraya had secretly replaced the eggs with two others, each inscribed with the names of Prince Ali and her daughter, Fanara. She hid the king's eggs and performed a fake ritual, asking everyone to close their eyes. When they opened them, she revealed the eggs with the names and declared, "The only way to save your kingdom is for Prince Ali to marry my daughter, Fanara."

King Rachad was suspicious but felt he had no choice. He agreed to the proposal, though his heart was heavy. When Prince Ali learned of the arrangement, he was horrified. "Father," he said, "I cannot marry Fanara. I do not love her, and I do not believe this prophecy. Please, give me time to find another solution."

The king, torn between his love for his son and his fear for the kingdom, reluctantly agreed. But he warned Ali, "Do not let your heart lead you astray. The fate of our people depends on this."

One evening, as Ali wandered through the city, he came across a young woman named Leila. She was beautiful, with a radiant smile and eyes that sparkled like the stars. But more than her beauty, Ali was struck by her kindness and intelligence. Leila came from a poor family, but her spirit was rich with wisdom and compassion. Ali felt an instant connection to her, and he knew in his heart that she was the one he wanted to marry.

He returned to the palace and told his father, "I have found the woman of my life, the future mother of this kingdom. Her name is Leila, and I love her."

King Rachad was stunned. "My son, how can you choose someone else over Fanara? Do you not care about the prophecy? Do you want to see the downfall of our kingdom?"

Ali stood firm. "Father, love is more powerful than any prophecy. Leila is the one who will bring strength and wisdom to our family. I cannot marry Fanara. My heart belongs to Leila."

The king, frustrated and fearful, insisted that Ali marry Fanara. But Ali refused, his resolve unshaken. He stopped eating and drinking, his love for Leila consuming him. The queen, Ali's mother, watched her son suffer and knew she had to intervene.

She approached King Rachad and said, "My love, our son is a slave to his heart. Love is more powerful than this kingdom. If we force him to marry against his will, we will lose him forever. Please, allow him to marry Leila. Trust that their love will bring prosperity, not ruin."

The king, moved by his wife's words and seeing the toll the situation had taken on Ali, finally relented. "Very well," he said. "Ali may marry Leila. But let us pray that this decision does not bring disaster upon us."

Ali, overjoyed, immediately went to Leila and proposed. She accepted, and their wedding was a grand celebration, filled with music, dancing, and laughter. The kingdom rejoiced, and as the years passed, it became clear that Ali and Leila's love was a blessing, not a curse.

Leila's wisdom and compassion made her a beloved queen, and together, she and Ali ruled with fairness and kindness. The kingdom flourished, becoming more powerful and prosperous than ever before. The people admired their rulers, and the bond between Ali and Leila became a symbol of true love and unity.

As for Zoraya, her deceit was eventually uncovered. She was banished from the kingdom, and her daughter, Fanara, chose to live a quiet life away from the palace. The kingdom learned that true power lies not in manipulation or fear, but in love, trust, and the courage to follow one's heart.

And so, Ali and Leila lived happily ever after, their love story inspiring generations to come. The kingdom thrived under their rule, a testament to the enduring power of love and the wisdom of those who dare to follow their hearts.

BETWEEN TWO HEARTS

*O*nce upon a time, in a bustling village nestled between rolling hills and fertile plains, there lived a man named Mdahoma. He was known for his wisdom, kindness, and unwavering faith in Allah. Mdahoma had married a woman named Lamina in his youth, a union that was initially filled with hope and promise. However, as the years passed, it became evident that Lamina had a harsh and unforgiving nature. Despite her difficult temperament, Mdahoma remained patient, believing that Allah would guide them through their trials.

After many years of marriage, Allah blessed Mdahoma and Lamina with several children. Mdahoma loved his children dearly and worked tirelessly to provide for them, but the strain of his marriage weighed heavily on his heart. Seeking solace and growth, Mdahoma made the difficult decision to leave his family temporarily and travel to a distant city to pursue further studies. He hoped that the time apart would bring clarity and peace to his troubled home.

In the new city, Mdahoma immersed himself in his studies, finding comfort in the pursuit of knowledge. It was there that he met Binti, a kind and gentle woman from his hometown. Binti's warmth and compassion stood in stark contrast to the harshness Mdahoma had endured for so long. Over time, their friendship blossomed into love, and Mdahoma, feeling far removed from the turmoil of his first marriage, decided to marry Binti. They were both from the same hometown, and Binti's understanding nature made her accepting of Mdahoma's past.

A year after their marriage, Allah blessed Mdahoma and Binti with a beautiful daughter. The child brought immense joy to their lives, and Mdahoma cherished every moment with his new family. However, he never forgot his responsibilities to his first wife and children. After completing his studies, Mdahoma decided it was time to return home and reunite with Lamina and his children.

When Mdahoma arrived home, he was met with a mixture of emotions. His children were overjoyed to see him, but Lamina's resentment had only grown in his absence. Mdahoma, hoping to be honest and transparent, informed Lamina about his second marriage to Binti. To his dismay, Lamina reacted with fury. She berated him, insulted him, and even resorted to physical violence.

Mdahoma, heartbroken and weary, endured her wrath for the sake of his children.

Years passed, and the tension in Mdahoma's home never subsided. Lamina's refusal to accept Binti and her constant hostility made life unbearable. In an attempt to bring peace, Mdahoma made the difficult decision to tell Lamina that he had divorced Binti. This lie temporarily eased the tension, but it came at a great cost. Mdahoma missed Binti and his daughter dearly, and the weight of his deception gnawed at his conscience.

One day, unable to bear the separation any longer, Mdahoma decided to visit Binti and his daughter. However, Lamina discovered his plans and blocked his path, refusing to let him leave. Her anger and jealousy knew no bounds, and she threatened to destroy any chance of reconciliation if he dared to go. Mdahoma, torn between his two families, felt trapped in a web of sorrow and regret.

Years of suffering and heartache followed. Mdahoma's spirit grew heavy with the burden of his divided life. Finally, he reached a breaking point. He decided to leave Lamina's home and move to a place where he could find peace and clarity. He settled in a quiet village, far from the chaos of his past, and began to rebuild his life.

When Lamina learned of Mdahoma's decision, she was consumed with rage. She stormed into his new home, demanding that he return to her. But Mdahoma stood firm. He told her that he would not go back unless she accepted the truth: he had two wives, and both deserved to be treated with respect and equality. He explained that his heart was big enough to love and care for both families, but he could no longer live in a world of lies and hostility.

Lamina, though initially resistant, began to see the pain she had caused. She realized that her jealousy and anger had driven Mdahoma away and had brought nothing but misery to their lives. Slowly, she started to soften, and though it was not easy, she agreed to accept the reality of Mdahoma's second marriage.

Mdahoma, grateful for this small step toward peace, worked tirelessly to ensure that both his families were treated fairly. He divided his time between them, ensuring that each wife and every child felt loved and valued. It was not a perfect arrangement, but it was built on honesty, respect, and a commitment to doing what was right.

In the end, Mdahoma's story became a tale of resilience, forgiveness, and the enduring power of love. He learned that true peace could only be found through honesty and equality, and he dedicated his life to upholding these principles. And so, Mdahoma's journey, though fraught with challenges, became a testament to the strength of the human spirit and the possibility of redemption.

FROM BETRAYAL
TO TRIUMPH

*O*nce upon a time, in a small but vibrant village surrounded by lush fields and rolling hills, there lived a young man named Nidwami. From the time he was a child, Nidwami dreamed of becoming the most successful and respected business expert in his village. He was known for his sharp mind, determination, and unwavering faith in Allah. His dream was not just to achieve personal success but to uplift his entire community through his knowledge and skills.

As Nidwami grew older, he realized that to achieve his dream, he needed to learn from the best. He decided to leave his village and travel to a powerful and prosperous kingdom, renowned for its wise scholars and thriving businesses. The journey was long and challenging, but

Nidwami's determination never wavered. When he arrived in the kingdom, he was in awe of its grandeur and the wealth of knowledge it offered. He immediately enrolled in a prestigious academy to study business and economics, dedicating himself to his studies with relentless focus.

Years passed, and Nidwami's hard work began to pay off. He became one of the top students at the academy, admired by his peers and mentors alike. One day, while attending a training session, he noticed a beautiful and intelligent woman named Amina. She was graceful, kind, and shared his passion for learning. Over time, their friendship deepened, and Nidwami found himself falling in love with her. With the blessings of their families and Allah, they married and began a new chapter of their lives together.

Nidwami was a devoted husband, caring for Amina and ensuring she lacked nothing. Allah blessed their union with a beautiful daughter, who inherited the best qualities of both her parents. The child was a perfect blend of her mother's grace and her father's wisdom, and she brought immense joy to their lives. For a time, Nidwami felt that his life was complete — he had a loving family, a successful career, and the respect of his peers.

However, Nidwami's thirst for knowledge was unquenchable. He decided to travel to Amina's homeland to further his studies and gain a deeper understanding of her culture and traditions. Though it was difficult to leave his family, Nidwami believed that this journey would ultimately benefit them all. He promised Amina that he would return as soon as his studies were complete.

Years passed, and Nidwami excelled in his studies, but his heart ached for his wife and daughter. He often thought of them, longing to hold them in his arms again. When he finally completed his studies, he eagerly returned home, expecting to be greeted with love and warmth. But to his dismay, things had changed.

Amina's behavior was cold and distant. She began to put immense pressure on Nidwami, criticizing him and creating unnecessary conflicts. Nidwami, being a wise and observant man, sensed that something was amiss. He suspected that Amina had grown close to someone else during his absence, but he chose not to confront her immediately. Instead, he watched and waited, hoping to understand the truth.

+ + +

Unbeknownst to Nidwami, Amina had indeed formed relationships with two other men. She no longer wanted to be married to Nidwami but feared the consequences of divorcing him, especially the disapproval of her mother. To force Nidwami's hand, she began to stay out late, claiming she was working. In reality, she spent her evenings with the other men, returning home only when the night was deep. Sometimes, she would travel to other cities under the guise of fieldwork, staying away for days or even weeks.

Nidwami, though heartbroken, remained patient. He continued to care for their daughter and maintained a calm demeanor, refusing to let his suspicions show. But Amina's pressure grew unbearable. She constantly picked fights, accused him of neglect, and made it clear that she no longer wanted to be with him. Finally, Nidwami realized that their marriage was beyond repair. With a heavy heart, he decided to leave Amina, choosing peace over a life of constant conflict.

Just one week after their separation, Amina married one of the men she had been seeing. While many in the village were shocked, Nidwami felt a sense of relief. He had endured years of emotional turmoil, and now he was free to rebuild his life. He returned to his homeland, where he was welcomed with open arms by his family and friends.

In time, Nidwami met a kind and respectful woman named Mwana Aisha. She was beautiful, both in appearance and character, and she brought warmth and joy back into Nidwami's life. They married with the blessings of their families, and Nidwami inherited his father's thriving business. Under his leadership, the business flourished, becoming one of the most successful enterprises in the region.

Nidwami and Mwana Aisha were blessed with many children, each one a testament to their love and devotion. Nidwami's dream of becoming the best business expert in his village had come true, but more importantly, he had found true happiness and peace. He often reflected on his journey, grateful for the lessons he had learned and the strength he had gained.

As for Amina, her life took a different path. Her hasty decisions and lack of integrity led to a series of struggles, and she often regretted the choices she had made. But Nidwami, ever the wise and compassionate man, harbored no ill will toward her. He prayed that she would find peace and happiness, just as he had.

And so, Nidwami's story became a tale of resilience, wisdom, and the enduring power of faith. He proved that even in the face of betrayal and heartbreak, one can rise above and create a life filled with love, success, and purpose. His legacy lived on, not just in his business, but in the hearts of his children and the community he had worked so hard to uplift.

9 798897 774616